CW00685311

Sleight ~~of Hand~~

in Deadwood

Karaoke, Cards, & Clutter Series
A Chic Lit story about Maribeth Thorp
A tale of friendship, love, trust, romance, and
life in general

Book #5

Lynn Donovan

Copyright

This book is a work of fiction. The names, characters, places, and incidents are all products of the author's imagination and are not to be construed as real. Any resemblances to persons, organizations, events, or locales are entirely coincidental.

The book contains material protected under International and Federal Copyright Laws and Treaties. All rights are reserved with the exceptions of quotes used in reviews. No part of this book may be reproduced or transmitted in any form or by any means, electronic or mechanical, including photocopying, recording, or by any information storage system without express written permission from the author.

This book was written by a human and not Artificial Intelligence (A.I.).

This book cannot be used to train Artificial Intelligence (A.I.).

About this Series

Karaoke, Cards, & Clutter Series

Maribeth Thorp is looking for a new start in Deadwood, South Dakota. Having left the boyfriend of eight years, she is desperate for a new beginning. Gambling on a house deed she won after a successful night of cards, she moves into the home on a blind bet. As things unfold, Maribeth finds herself in one dilemma after another. Can she resolve life's unexpected surprises and maintain her sanity at the same time? Or will it all come crashing down on top of her in one giant epic failure?

Introduction

Sleight of Hand in Deadwood

Maribeth Thorp may wreak havoc on the gaming
tables, but she's not a home wrecker. When she's
accused of having an affair with another woman's
husband, Maribeth sets out to expose the wife's true
intentions and save the husband's reputation. That's
nothing compared to the threat hovering over her
friend's life. Now that she and the detective have an
understanding, she will have to use a sleight of hand
to rescue her friend and take her relationship with
the detective to the next level? Will it be a total trick
or just an illusion?

Acknowledgements

Thank you to everybody in my life who has contributed in one way or another to the writing of this book. My husband, my children, my children-in-law, and my grandchildren. You all are my unconditional fans. My BETA reader and grammar guru who make me look gooder than I am. [Bad grammar intended.] My fellow author friends who chat with me daily to exchange ideas, encourage, maintain sanity, and keep me from being a total recluse/hermit.

Mostly I thank God for the talent he has given me. I hope to hear you say, "Well done, my good and faithful servant," when I cross the Jordan and run into your arms—Many, many years from now. :)..

Chapter One

"Do you think we will find a *golden nugget* like you did in Miss Timberly's basement?" Wild William, one of the owners of Deadwood Tobacco Company, asks with sparkling hope in his caramel eyes.

When Tricia Timberly and I decluttered her basement full of her maternal and paternal grandparents' belongings, she found a painting by an Italian artist from the fifteenth century. Her grandfather had been with a brigade who saved some precious artwork from a fire set by Nazi soldiers. Seems somehow ol' grandpa managed to sneak this one home inside a mattress that was shipped with a German hand-carved bedroom suite.

I just smile at William's expectant expression. Everybody hopes for that one forgotten item that is worth a fortune among their stuff. Most times, it's just stuff. The only real value is what the person places on its memory.

The tobacco company's basement is filled with old furniture and what-not from when Wild William and his partners moved the shop from an East Main Street location to this West Main Street location.

"We never know what treasures we might find," I answer as I always do. Wild William puffs his long, mud-colored Padron cigar, sending streamers of smoke toward the ceiling between us. He brought me one of my favorite cigars, a Blue Star Number one, when he greeted me this morning, but I haven't unwrapped it yet. I'll wait for when we take a break and smoke it with him then. Knowing Wild William, this cigar he is smoking will not be the only one he cuts and lights today.

Today, I am standing under the tobacco shop in a different basement from where I've been before. This section is under the front of the store and is filled nearly to the rafters with boxes, old tables and chairs, and God only knows what else. Wild William, Randall, and Allen, the co-owners, bought new furnishings for the new location and stored the older stuff down here with the typical thought that they would do something with it "someday."

The back section of the basement that I am more familiar with is where I have taken part in a few high-stakes poker games when I needed some extra money. The first time was when I moved here with nothing but my shampoo, a toothbrush, a cappuccino machine, and a deed to a house on Williams Street after my separation from Jason Rumbar. Our eight-year, dead-end relationship was tapped out and so were my finances.

Today is that "someday" for these guys to do something with this stuff. I will take a *before* picture and begin the process of working with them to reduce, reuse, or recycle. It is too bad I wasn't here when they moved to this location. I could have saved them a lot of packing and moving had I been able to assist with the sifting and sorting.

No matter.

I'm here now. They have hired me to help. Of course, the hopes of finding something outrageously valuable is always a great incentive for cleaning out a space. Now that word is out about Tricia having a gold mine in her basement, I have become a highly sought after Celebrity Personal

Organizer. At least in Deadwood. I am booked solid for months.

In fact, I've been so busy with one declutter after another I have hardly had time to see Blaze, the guy next door who makes my heart gallop in circles. Our relationship is building, I think, I might could even call him my boyfriend, but I don't want to jinx anything.

With a new vintage puppy living with me, who had medical needs, it has been great having Blaze next door and working nights. He is able to see that Retired Sargent-Major Barkley has his pills and is well cared for while I'm at work during the day. He even sees to the dog's hottub therapy since he bought a spa-tub for his backyard, claiming he had wanted one all along but bought it for Barkley's needs.

Blaze fostered Barkley initially when the dog's human partner died suddenly, and the malamute needed a new forever home. The retired military-turned-police dog chose me for that long-term commitment when a man I knew as Uncle Donald attacked me in an effort to overtake the local underground gambling operation here in Deadwood. Barkley saved my life, and I promised him I'd make the rest of his as happy as I possibly could.

Smiling at Wild William, I pretend to roll up imaginary sleeves and say, "Let's get to work."

We go out to the alley where I explain the three-tarp process. Three tarps are laid out. Ian, the youngest salesman in the shop, stands guard over the three spots since it is in the alley and who knows what or who might try to get into whatever we set out there. Wild William listens to my instructions, but he seems distracted.

"Yeah, yeah, yeah," The gold rings on each of his fingers reflect the afternoon sun as his hand rolls in a gesture for me to finish my spiel. "And where do we put the goods that's gonna get me some real dough?"

I smile. "We'll cross that bridge when we get there." I look around. "But if we think we have something delicate or special, we'll pull out another tarp or blanket and put the items on it. When Trish found those Precious Moments—"

"Yeah, yeah." He turns his back on me. "Who cares about some unholy dust catchers, I want the good stuff!" He growls as he leads the way back to the storage basement.

"Well, aren't you the one who packed all that stuff before it got stored downstairs?" I shake my head as I walk behind him. We walk through the shop on our way to the basement stairs.

"I wasn't the only one. We all worked on it." He frowned. "I don't know *everything* that's down here."

I roll my eyes. When we reach the bottom of the floor, he smiles an ornery grin. If I didn't know better, I'd think he was grinning at me with lustful thoughts. But I do know better. He's lusting after the possibility of some real cash. As I walk behind him, I shake my head in wonder. We've got a long day ahead of us. It may end with a great deal of disappointment, or it may end with jubilation over something we find. Who knows?

We each lift a box and carry it to the alley. Wild William cuts the tape and begins going through the contents. While I walk back to the basement. Allen follows me down.

"I've got some time, Maribeth," he says.

"We can use the help." I smile at him. Together, we start hauling up boxes, filling a box dolly, and taking them to Wild William to sort. We get a good rhythm going and get a lot done until noon.

"Ready for lunch?" I ask Wild William on my last trek to the alley.

"Sure." He pants. His face is beet red, and a sheen of sweat covers his sparsely covered head, face, and neck.

"You look like you need a break anyway." I say. "Are you drinking water?"

"Naw, I don't need water. I'm fine." He stands and straightens his back. He seems a little off balance. "I'm fine." He repeats, then his eyes roll up and his knees give out. He collapses.

"I need some help out here!" I scream and run to his side.

Randall runs into the alley with a small bottle of orange juice. He is twisting the top as he runs to William's side. "Prop him up" Randall squats beside his partner.

I do as ordered and shove William's shoulders, supporting him against my knee. Randall put the orange juice bottle to William's lips. "Come on buddy, you need to drink this." He coos.

"What's wrong with him?" I ask.

"His blood sugar dips sometimes. This juice will help." Randall tips the bottle slowly allowing William to sip the sugary contents.

"What could have happened if we hadn't been out here when he passed out?" I ask.

Randall shrugs. "He could have gone into a diabetic coma, or simply died. Dang fool, he knows better." He says while continuing to make William sip the orange juice.

The color in William's face resumes a normal hue and his eyes stop rolling in their sockets. He focuses straight ahead as if there were someone or thing standing there. "What happened?"

"You didn't check your blood sugar today, you moron." Randal fusses at William the only way two life-long friends can.

William's face draws up like a morning glory in daylight. "I did too, you ugly old goat. It's just that I didn't eat no breakfast."

"Good night nurse, Will! You know better than to skip a meal!" Randall puts the lid back on the empty bottle and stands. "Why don't you come inside and let me fix you a cheese sandwich while Allen comes out here and does" —his eyes rove over the three tarps and the items separated on each one— "Whatever this is you are doing."

Ian steps closer. "He's on a treasure hunt, like Tricia Timberly."

Randall's lips curl into a frown to the side of his face. "Yeah, well, the dang fool nearly found the pearly gates instead of an earthly treasure."

They laugh.

"I can go through the boxes, Randall." Ian says. "I know what system Wild William was using."

"Okay, you take over here." Randall turns to me. "I need to be inside, but I'll send Allen out to help you."

I nod. "Are you sure William is alright?"

"Yeah," Randall shakes his head. "I'll make sure he takes his insulin and he'll be finer than frog's hair."

I chuckle. "Okay. If you're sure."

Randall gives me a smile. "I'm sure."

Allen steps to the door leading into the alley. "Maribeth." He searches the faces as if he's looking for mine. "There's someone here to see you."

My heart turns a little summersault. Is it Blaze? "Who is it?" I ask just for good measure.

Allen shrugs. "I don't know. She said she needs to speak to you about Frank."

"Frank?" I stand. "Who would want to talk to me about Frank... Except... Oh no!"

Chapter Two

Kate is ringing her long fingers as if she were trying to get the last drop of blood out of each digit while standing behind a well-dressed, dark-skinned woman I do not know. This has to be Millie Holmes. Who else would be here asking about Frank?

Kate, known locally as Crazy Kate, had dyed her previously pink bangs to an olive green. I suppose to match her Army Surplus tropical-green utility vest, cotton t-shirt, and ruched cargo pocketed pants. Except for the black and white canvas Converse shoes and red Betty Boop socks, she is head to toe Army. It's not crazy to wear army surplus, but for Kate, it does perpetuate her reputation for being different. It's what I love about her the most.

The woman with Kate waits just inside the front door of the tobacco shop as if she would be more comfortable in a Lane Bryant clothing store than this male-dominate sort of store. Kate waits behind her as if etiquette does not allow her to walk ahead of the royal figure she has delivered. I walk up to them maintaining a relaxed posture and tone. Allen veers off into the humidor busying himself with tidying up the shelves. I figure he's giving me privacy to talk.

Or does he know what is about to go down?

The woman glares at me with disdain and purpose in her eyes, while Kate continues to be fidgety, almost erratic. Is she preparing to take off at any second? I smile at the woman. Her meticulous makeup, perfectly chosen for her creamy-mocha skin, has a wilted appearance as if she has been exposed to the heat far too long. Her blue-green box-hat sits slightly askew in her nest of dark wavy curls.

Dressed as if ready for church, rather than a challenge, in a tricolor of blue, green, and gold waffle tweed suit-dress. The hem of her sleeve cuts into her flaccid bicep. Either the tailor should have used more material to make the suit jacket fit properly or this woman has gained weight since she bought it. Regardless, she holds herself and her chin high with dignity. Her nose, once powdered, but now glistens with beads of perspiration and little remnant clumps of face powder, is the path in which her eyes target me.

Who is this woman? Why does Kate look as though she has brought me Satan's wife for a declutter of hades consultation?

My eyes flit to Kate and back to the fuming-faced woman.

"How can I help you?" I ask, sweeter than my momma's coconut custard pie.

Her full, lower lip quivers. The cherry-red lipstick has faded or is chewed off except for the edges of her mouth. The color of pale-pink skin on her lips shows through.

"I am Mildred Holmes," she says as if that should tell me everything I need to know.

I pause a moment. Mildred Holmes? "You're Millie?" I decipher.

I only know Frank's wife as Millie. That's the only thing he has ever called her. Frank is the previous owner of my house. I won the deed from Frank at a poker game in Vegas. This is Millie! The woman who throws him out of their house in Dallas, Texas, whenever his luck runs dry and he comes home to her empty handed?

Before I moved here, Frank would come to Deadwood to seek refuge in their vacation home, now my house, here in Deadwood until Millie cooled down and allowed him to return home. When I finally came here to claim ownership, Frank showed up one night, thinking I would never actually move in, even though he had lost the right to ownership.

It scared the bejeezies out of me to find Frank standing in my living room that first night. Thank goodness, Blaze was quick to stick his nose in and take Frank under his strong arm to guide him over to his house next door. Frank still shows up from time to time. Seeking refuge from his furious wife. I've come to terms with Frank's need to lay low. It's my way to pay-it-forward, because I remember well what it was like for Momma and me when we had nowhere to turn, when Daddy lost everything and took his life.

Frank and I have a friendship of sorts. He can stay a night or two at my house as long as he doesn't break in. I'd prefer he stay with Blaze, but I also know Blaze is seldom home at night when

Frank shows up in Deadwood. I have even designated the extra-guest bedroom in my house for Frank when he needs it. It's on the opposite side of the house from my bedroom and has a separate bathroom, giving us both privacy. And he knows to ring the doorbell rather than jimmy the lock at my front door.

Apparently, *Mildred Holmes* has come to Deadwood, but why? She is looking for Frank? But is she seeking time alone at the house she thinks is her vacation home? How did she know where I was today? Or that I existed at all?

"Oh." I mutter to myself. Of course, Kate wouldn't think twice about telling anybody where I am when or if they ask for a taxi ride to my house and find it to be void of me… or Frank.

I put out my hand. "I'm Maribeth Thorp. What can I do for you?"

She stares at my hand as if I am shoving a venomous snake toward her. Lifting her face, she rolls her eyes up to meet mine. "I am looking for my husband."

I feign confusion, then fake realization. "Oh! You're Frank's wife."

I really should receive an Oscar for my performance. Instead, I get a hard look from her.

"Yes, I am. And you are the little tater tot he's been coming here to see when I… when he and I need time to evaluate our priorities." She chose her words very carefully.

"I, uh, I'm not sure what you think Frank has been doing when he comes here, but…" I stammer. Does she realize they don't own the house on Williams Street anymore? "I take it you are looking for him but he wasn't" —I clear my throat — "there?"

I glance at Kate who mouths "sorry," and sort of curtsies.

Mrs. Holmes presses her lips together. "Yes." She lifts that round chin another notch. "No. He was not there. It seems the locks have been changed."

She gestures toward Kate with a blue, summer cotton gloved hand. "This kind taxi driver was gracious enough to help me locate… *you*." She said the word *you* like it soured on her tongue as it passed over to escape through her lips. "Please tell me where my Frank is." Her tone changes to an almost pleading rather than angry sound.

My mouth drops open. I had to think what on earth I should say. In the end I decided on the truth. "I… honestly don't know."

I figure we can sort out her misunderstanding of my role in Frank's escaping here from time to time later, after she has calmed down enough to actually discuss this situation.

Tears redden her eyes but her chin juts out with intentional loftiness. "Well, if you don't know, who does?"

I shrug. My eyes lift to Kate who looks ill. Concern for her clenches my heart but I return my attention to Mrs. Holmes. "Perhaps Blaze."

"Blaze? What is a blaze?"

I smile. "Blaze is m— the neighbor."

"Neighbor?" The skin between her brows move slightly, as if she intended to draw them together but the last botox injection still has a paralyzing effect. "OH! You mean Jonathan Hemingway, that skinny detective with greying temples. Yes, he seemed friendly enough— but why would Frank… why would he know where my Frank is when you—?"

I tilt my head to the side. "Mrs. Holmes, I'm not who you think I am."

Her brows lift along with her forehead as if it were all one solid object attached to the top half of her face. "Oh, really?" She says in a high-pitched, goose-like voice. She sounds like Miss

Prissy, the bonnet wearing goose from the Looney Toons cartoon with Foghorn Leghorn as her person of interest. A romantic interest, I say. I'm hearing Foghorn's distinctive southern dialect in my head.

I glance at Kate. Her pallor is not improving. "Kate, are you alright?"

Kate bobs her head but staggers back like she is standing in a carnival fun house where the floorboards keep moving under her feet. I move toward her to steady her. "Kate?"

Kate's spindly knees bend and she goes down just out of my reach.

"Oh, gosh!" I lunge to help her. "William!" I yell. "Allen! Randall! Anybody!"

Mrs. Holmes squats next to Kate, her thick thighs strain the hem of her knee-length dress. She takes her taxi driver's wrist and wraps her long, large fingers around, then looks at the watch on her left arm. She pats Kate's arm as she lays it across Kate's middle. "You heart rate is a little fast, hon." She touched Kate's forehead. "Are you diabetic?"

Diabetic! This is the second time today this subject has come up. I ponder the likelihood of such a coincidence.

Kate shakes her head.

Mrs. Holmes smiles. "Could you be pregnant?"

Kate vehemently shakes her head and her eyes bulge with a new layer of fear.

I almost laugh, but the seriousness of Kate nearly passing out holds my giggle back, like a National Guard soldier blocking a protestor. I watched as Mrs. Holmes continued to assess Kate's weakened state. I honestly figure I know what is wrong with her. She's terrified she has brought me trouble. I'm not mad at her. Although I wish she'd remember to act a little less *knowledgeable* of my whereabouts when someone she doesn't know asks for me, but I'm not mad.

I squat on the opposite side of Kate and lean in so only she can hear me. "Kate, it's alright that you brought Mrs. Holmes to me."

Kate looks deeply into my eyes as tears pool along her bottom lashes. "You sure?" she utters.

"Yes, I'm sure." I say.

Kate moves to stand. I help her to her feet. Mrs. Holmes fusses about her staying put and is shoving a small can of orange juice from behind the bar into Kate's hand even though she told the woman she was not diabetic. I hug Kate once she's standing.

When my friend stands at her full height, she is taller than me— and I'm five-foot-nine. Her long gangly arms and legs give her an appearance of the cartoon character, Olive Oyl, Popeye's girlfriend. However, for some reason, she always slumps forward making her look shorter than me. I don't know if she's embarrassed about her height or has weak bones. Right now, she stands slightly above me by two inches and is smiling like she did when she won twenty-five-thousand dollars at the karaoke contest in the Buffalo Bodega Complex.

To this day she does not realize the contest was rigged for her to win. I had tried to give her twenty-thousand dollars from my surplus winnings after an underground poker game so she could have a downpayment to buy her house. Her landlord had decided to sell their rental property and Kate didn't want to leave the home she had rented and loved for so long.

Kate had refused to accept my financial gift, so the girls; Tricia, Cindy , Michelle, Suzie, and I pooled our *extra* funds, making the pot twenty-five-thousand and arranged for her to win it at the Buffalo Bodega's karaoke contest. She is a happy homeowner now and none the wiser of our fixed involvement.

I lean up to hug her and whisper, "it's okay," in her ear.

She squeezes me a little tighter and whispers, "Good," with a little hitch in her voice. Mrs. Holmes looks flabbergasted with her jaw hanging open. "Were you faking it all along?"

Kate and I both turn in surprise. "No!" we say at the same time.

I continue to hold Kate but say to Mrs. Holmes, "She was overwhelmed with concern… about bringing you here."

"But… she's a taxi driver, why would bringing me here be so much of a concern to her that she would pass out?"

I pinched my lips between my teeth and thought about how to explain this to the woman. "I, uh, well, you see…"

"I knew where Maribeth was," Kate jumped on the explanation for me,. "because I know her car and saw it when I drove by to pick you up at the Rapid City airport. Legally, I should not have brought you here when we went to the house and you asked where you could find her."

I suppress a giggle. Legally, Kate should not be pretending to be a taxi driver.

"I see." Mrs. Holmes crosses her beefy arms over her abundant chest. "So, you two are friends?"

"Well, yes." I say. "You and I can be friends, too, if you want." I smile in an attempt to seal this friendship deal.

Mrs. Holmes draws herself up, although she looks no taller than five-foot-three, and moves the plate upward that holds her frozen eyebrows. "Why, would I want to be friends with the woman who is trying to steal my husband away from me?"

"Wha—" Kate and I both gape at her.

Finally, I stammer, "I'm not— I think you— Mrs. Holmes, we really need to talk."

Chapter Three

It is a bit of a surprise to me that I don't see Frank's red Jeep Wrangler in my drive or Blaze's. If Mrs. Holmes is hunting him down, and he's not here, where has he gone? Do they own other property that he might seek refuge in while his wife calms down? I glance at Blaze's house as I roll past and pull into my driveway. His garage door is opening, but the garage is empty. That's when I notice his gladiator is behind Kate's Bronco in our procession down the street.

He's just getting home.

My heart flutters at the thought of being close to him. Any excuse to see my handsome neighbor sends a thrill down my spine, ending at my toes. A smile tingles on my lips in anticipation of a kiss from him. I will ask him if he's heard from Frank, then maybe steal a kiss. That ought to show Mrs. Holmes I have a beau and am not after her husband.

Kate's Bronco pulls in behind me. The midday sun reflects off the shiny, metallic trim that frames the black letters of her "Taxi" placard, hanging by a suction cup on her windshield under her rearview mirror, and reflects a mirror-ball effect on the numbers above my garage door. Kate, more commonly known around Deadwood as Crazy Kate because of her eccentricities, is not a legitimate taxi driver, nor is she an Uber driver, but she has placards for both. The City of Deadwood does not allow Uber services and the one taxi service has an online site where one can easily request a taxi.

I've never quite figured out how Kate does it, but apparently she is a bit of a genius when it comes to computers and hacking into the local online services. My friend, good ol' Crazy Kate, knows how to tap into the website's request form and if she beats the legitimate taxi driver to the customer, the customer is none the wiser once they are in the backseat of her moss-green Bronco. Much like myself when Kiley was broken down I had no idea Kate wasn't legit.

Sure, there were clues, obvious ones, now that I look back. Her interchangeable placards that she sticks to her windshield, for one, and the fact that she only takes cash. Then there was the quickly-spoken advice when she was approached downtown by a police officer to not mention I had paid her for the ride. I can't explain it really, but all these things endeared Kate to me, once I figured out she wasn't a dangerous sociopath. We are good friends to this day.

I couldn't bring myself to tell Mrs. Holmes that Frank and she no longer own the house I now live in while we were at the Deadwood Tobacco Company store. So, I suggested we go to *the* house — I intentionally used the generic article "the" instead of a possessive pronoun "my" or "your" when referring the house— where we can sit down and talk this through. I had hoped, maybe when we got there, Frank would be waiting and he could clear this whole thing up.

Blaze pulls into his garage. I pray he comes back out once he gets parked. Being the nosey neighbor that he is, he usually notices when things are askew. I wasn't sure if I should signal him, somehow. Should I text him? He had once told me to flash my porch light to let him know, much like the bat signal calling the superhero into action. Being that I'm not inside my house, I cannot flicker my porch light. And to flash my high beams would be too obvious.

He would be the perfect ally for when I explain to Mrs. Holmes why I'm living here. He knew the whole story about Frank and his losing this house to me in a poker game. When I first came here to claim my house, Blaze bulldozed in wanting to know who I was. Then Frank arrived, unexpectedly, late in the evening, scaring a week of Sunday's out of me. Blaze showed up and saved my dignity and Frank's when he offered his couch to Frank until the poor boy could go back home.

Barkley sounded his alarm, barking at my front door. I wasn't too sure how Mrs. Holmes would react to my vintage puppy, Retired Sergeant Major Barkley. He is a large Malamute who loves everybody as long as they are not trying to hurt me. But not everybody is comfortable around large dogs.

Thank goodness all my fears are put to rest when Blaze steps out of his garage. I make eye contact with him before I lead Mrs. Holmes to the three flights of wooden stairs where my front door is located. Will the heavy-set woman be able to climb so many steps and live to tell about it? Wait, what was I thinking? This had been *her* vacation home. Surely, she's aware of the only path to the front door?

"Hey!" I call to him in a neighborly fashion.

"Hey," he answers. His eyes flit from me to Kate's late model Bronco, then Mrs. Holmes emerging from the back seat. I see understanding clearing in his previously cloudy-with-confusion eyes.

I open my mouth to introduce the woman to him, but—

"Hey, Millie!" He rushes across the yard to Mrs. Holmes who is straightening the taut hem across her thick knees.

—Apparently, he already knows her!

"How are you?" He hugs her like they are old friends.

At the Deadwood Tobacco Company she acted like she barely knew him. Even calling him Jonathan Hemingway, as if they had met once, the way neighbors do. Now they act like old chums. I stood with my eyebrows knitted together watching this exchange.

"I, uh, take it you know each other?" I ask more than say.

"Oh, sure." Blaze gives Mrs. Holmes a squeeze. "Are you looking for Frank?"

"Yes." Tears choke her word. "Oh, Jonathan, I'm afraid I was just awful to him this time."

Wait a second! Nobody who is this *friendly* with Blaze calls him by his Christian name. When I first met him, he told me all his friends call him Blaze. They certainly seem like friends to me. Why is she not calling him by his nickname?

She dabs a long fingernail sideways under her heavily mascara-covered lower lashes to catch her tear before it streaks what's left of her makeup. The heat and humidity have already done a pretty good job of making her foundation cover-up disappear.

"Well, Millie," Blaze holds her by the shoulders. "You have warned him repeatedly."

I stare at them, forgetting to close my mouth until I feel saliva roll over my lip. I gulp and smack my lips, bringing myself and my manners back into alignment. "Uh, Mrs. Holmes?"

I meet Blaze's gaze with an exaggerated wide-eyed attempt to convey my concern for Mrs. Holmes presence, how she does not know about me owning the house, and that he and she seems to be such good friends.

I speak to the people standing in my driveway in my usual professional manner. "Let's go inside and see what we can do to help you find Frank."

Blaze smiles at me then turns to Mrs. Holmes. "Sure, let's go inside."

Kate begins to fidget again. "I, uh, have another call," she states although I never saw her lift her phone to look at the screen.

I nod, giving her the okay to take off, then lead the way up the stairs. Barkley sends us his welcome-home greeting through the door in a loud, wolf-like howl. I don't dare look back to see how Mrs. Holmes is reacting to the sound of his deep bark. When I unlock the two locks that Blaze installed for my added security and open my front door, I immediately speak to Barkley. "Sit."

He obeys, but his tail wags and he shifts on his front paws with obvious excitement. I love his little dance. I pat his head. "Good boy."

I look back to see if Mrs. Holmes is alright with the stairs and/or Barkley. She is breathing hard, like I do when I make my way up the three flights, but she seems okay.

I move past my dog, secretly wishing his growl would run Mrs. Holmes off for good, but Barkley sits obediently, albeit excitedly.

"Can I get you anything? Water, Wine."

She hisses at me. "I do not drink the devil's piss!"

Whoa! Language! I think, but do not say.

Blaze enters behind Mrs. Holmes. "Now, Millie. You know Jesus turned water into wine, it's not devil's piss. All things in moderation."

She puckers her no-longer-lipstick-covered lips as if she has eaten a sour pickle and shrugs one shoulder. "That's not how I was raised."

"I know." He turns to me. "Water for both of us, Maribeth."

I tilt my head, considering this different man that stands before me from the Blaze I knew prior to now. Even Barkley turns his head, analyzing this new Blaze.

"Okay." I say.

I take three bottles of water from the fridge and set them on the coffee table as Blaze sits next to Mrs. Holmes on the couch. Signaling Barkley to relax and come sit beside me with a pat on my thigh, I sit in the chair. He sits as instructed and pants.

Having Blaze as an ally seems to be working. Mrs. Holmes doesn't seem to be nearly as riled up as before. She sniffs.

"Oh, Jonathan, is Frank cheating on me… with her?" She finishes her words out of the side of her mouth as if that would hide them from my hearing, then cuts a sharp-as-a-dagger look at me.

"Noooo!" Blaze chuckles. "This is Maribeth Thorp. She…"

His gaze snaps to me. As if he suddenly realizes why I am so concerned about Mrs. Holmes being here. "She is here because…"

I jump in. "Frank and I worked out an… arrangement." It's not a lie. We did work out an amicable agreement. I own the house, he does not, but when he is desperate, he can come crash here until Mrs. Holmes calms down.

Mrs. Holmes's eyes focus on me. She blinks. "You mean… Frank is letting you rent the place?"

I really don't want to lie to the woman. I don't want to tell her she no longer owns this house either… so I twist the truth. "Frank is… uh, Frank and I have agreed it's okay for me to live here." I say. A smile quivers at the corners of my mouth. I'm rather proud of my twisted version of the truth.

"Yeah," Blaze backs me up. "That's the truth."

Mrs. Holmes looks between us, as if we were tossing a ball back and forth. "What are you not telling me, Jonathon?"

Blaze and I gawk at each other.

Since I've been on a roll with Lady Luck looking over my shoulder, I say, "Nothing."

Mrs. Holmes's eyes narrow as they slide over to me. "Oh, really?"

She stands, planting her hands on her abundant hips, and turns to face Blaze. "Jonathan, tell me the truth! Why is this woman living in my vacation home?"

Blaze sighs. "Millie, the truth is—"

The front door opens. Barkley growls, lowering his front end. We all turn to see who is walking in.

Shit fire and save the matches! I leap to my feet. "What are you doing… where are your clothes?" Frank stands in my foyer barefoot and wrapped in a beach towel.

Mrs. Holmes wails, "Oh, Frank! Where have you been? I'm so happy to find you!"

Frank's dark skin pales to a dark ashen, hollow appearance. His eyes widen and his jaw goes lax. "Uh, Millie?"

I put my open palm in front of Barkley's face to instruct him to stay. "Frank? Have you been in Blaze's hot tub?"

He nods but confusion is still written all over his face.

Mrs. Holmes moves toward Frank, wrapping her arms around his neck, pulling him down to her lack of height and kisses him all over his face. If she still had that bright red lipstick, he'd be covered in red lip prints. "I'm so sorry, Frank. Please forgive me."

Apparently, his state of undress doesn't affect her enthusiasm.

I couldn't help but notice Frank didn't pucker or kiss her back. That seems odd to me. He is always so upset when he comes here to wait out her temper. Why isn't he thrilled she has come after him? Why does he look so indifferent?

Chapter Four

Diamond Lil's is crammed full with late-lunch diners. With tourism at its peak in Deadwood, the downtown restaurants were busy from open to close without the usual lull in the afternoon. I look across the sea of heads to find the one I came here to meet. Abbie Salvador, website designer extraordinaire, should be easy to find in the crowd of diners with her pink-tinted blond hair, although with tourist season, the influx of unusual people has every imaginable hair style and coloring.

I look for the person matching her headshot from her website where I requested a consult. I hope she can recognize me from my pitiful website headshot, which is actually a random selfie that I thought was good enough. She wiggles her fingers at me, and I tip my head back acknowledging I see her.

Diamond Lil's hostess grins at me. I smile at her. "Thank you, I see my friend."

She hesitates, but allows me to walk past the two-foot-by-two-foot sign clearly instructing patrons to wait to be seated. She hands me a menu and gestures for me to continue. I appreciate that she takes her job very seriously, and smile back at her, tucking the menu under my arm. Her job done, she returns to her post.

"Abbie?" I say as I reach the table. She stands with a nod. She's wearing dark pink waffle-spandex leggings under a Tinker Bell t-shirt that somehow looks adorable and professional at the same time. When she extends her arm to shake my hand, I see a Tinker Bell tattoo on her bicep. While slightly shorter than me, not unusual for me at five-foot-nine, she is tall for a woman and slender with obvious muscle tone in her arms. Apparently, in her perfect world, she has time to work out, too. I pull out the chair across from her and we both sit.

"I'm so glad you called," I say.

I need a website developer to help me expand my personal organizer business. Business is good in Deadwood, since local word-of-mouth has me scheduled out for several months, but I know from experience that won't carry me through to next year.

I submitted a request for a consult from her website when I saw that she was located in Rapid City. I need an online presence that brings it home when a customer reaches out, looking for help decluttering a space, and I wanted to be able to sit down and talk face-to-face rather than an on-screen meeting. I need someone local like Abbie who knows how to design a visually appealing website that has appropriate meta tags to put me at the top of search engines and functional landing pages with reliable contact forms, not to mention, working pop-up ads that stir interest, and other things I haven't thought of, because I'm not a website developer.

Her website did all that when I searched for a website developer, so I know she knows what she's doing.

"Thank you for meeting me so soon." I say as we lift our menus. She has no idea what a mess she pulled me out of back home. When she called, I was never so happy to receive an excellent excuse to exit stage left in the drama that was taking place in my living room. With Blaze present, I was able to delegate the whole scene of confusion to him with a promise to make it up to him later. Besides, he knew Frank and his wife way better than I. If anybody could resolve the problem between them, I was confident he could.

"Oh, I'm happy to help," she says with a pink-glossy-lips smile.

Three guesses what her favorite color is? She sounds like me when I meet a potential client. Her pink fixation gives her an air of eccentricity. I like her already.

Our waitress slips up to us asking for our drink order. A curtain of ash-blond hair tumbles over her eyes. What I assume was once a well gathered chignon, is now a fringe-framed messy bun come loose. We go ahead and tell her what we want to eat as well since the restaurant is so busy. I confess to Abbie that I'm pretty hungry, and she confesses she had forgotten to eat at noon, so this was good that we met for a late lunch.

Who forgets to eat? I ponder for a moment. But then, Abbie begins our meeting by opening her laptop with Tinker Bell stickers grouped over the front cover hiding the singular bitten apple emblem and turns the screen toward me. Similar to my scrap-book-style portfolio, she shows me her previous customers' before-and-after results of her work. I am already impressed by the website where I found her, but seeing other examples of her work seals my commitment to hire her. Pink preoccupation, Tinker Bell obsession, and all! I really like this gal.

"Here's the 'hard copy' of my portfolio." I show her my before-and-after examples in my well designed, scrapbook-style notebook just as our food arrives. Her laptop is shoved to the area where a third person would sit to my left, and my portfolio is shoved to the area to my right where a fourth would sit. We eat while discussing so many possibilities that she proposes to do for my business website. My excitement grows with each mouthful of food I consume.

Then Abbie opens her laptop and brings up her cost sheet which is at the end of her online presentation. My joy-bubble pops over my head and showers down disappointment-pebbles. I feel pummeled and bruised.

I can't afford her help.

My brain instantly jumps to the solution that always saves my butt in times of financial need— a high-stakes game. But I promised Blaze, when he brought me home after the raid on Big Mike's basement, that I would stop attending illegally hosted poker games.

Uncle Donald had forced me to take him to Big Mike's and he had bullied Mike into a corner with his take-over plan when Blaze and his team stormed into the basement. It had been an awful ordeal. While it wasn't my fault, I feel like I betrayed my friend, Big Mike, by bringing Uncle Donald unannounced and with hostile intentions. Then to have Blaze and his team raid the place—

I stunned Blaze when he found me at a table with cards in my hand and actively playing. While I was not breaking the law, it certainly was a strain on our potential relationship putting a wedge between him and I. Only by promising him I'd quit attending the poker games could I imagine he would continue to pursue getting to know me better. At least that was how I had processed everything. I have yet to know for certain if he is still interested in me.

Uncle Donald got what was coming to him and is now in prison. Big Mike received probation for turning state's witness against Donald who had forcefully taken over Mike's gaming lair the very night that the vigilante detectives busted in to put a stop to everything.

My knee-jerk response to needing a lot of money is a moot idea since, as far as I know, there are no high-stakes underground games going on in Deadwood anymore. And if there were, would I be as *lucky* as I have always been without Donald's heavy-handed assurance for my winning?

I know the chances I take every time I turn to a high-stakes game, and the consequences should I lose. At least I suspect the consequences would be the same for me as they were for my daddy— insanity, resolved by suicide. Or was there more to my dad's choice to end his life? Did Donald have something to do with Daddy's death? The question continues to niggle at my brain.

I chew my lip, worrying over everything tumbling in my brain. How can I possibly pay Abbie for these services that I truly need and not risk my sanity to acquire the funds. I lift my eyes and realize she is staring at me.

Concern, or is it panic, shows loud and clear in her tight jaw. She swallows. Her lips part and she acts like she wants to say something. She licks her lips. "Do you…" She starts again. "Do you ever exchange service for service?"

My eyes pop open. "You mean… like I help someone declutter their space and they do something for me without exchanging money?"

She bites her pink glossy lower lip and nods.

Could it be possible that she has a cluttered basement somewhere and needs my services? "Yes, absolutely. What do you have in mind?"

Relief washes over her like a bucket of warm water poured down her back. I know how she feels. I'm feeling it too.

"Oh, good." She giggles. "Because when I saw your inquiry and looked over your website for an idea of what you needed, I was really hoping we could work out a swap." She grins with a look of hope that I always love to see in my potential customers' faces.

"You worked up an estimate for me. Let's go look at what you are needing, and I'll work up an estimate for you. I'm sure we can work out a plan," I say.

"When can you come to my house?" she asks.

"In the wise words of Ben Franklin, 'Never leave until tomorrow which you can do today.' How about I follow you to your place?"

As an answer to me, she waves at our waitress. "Check please!"

We turn off Main Street and then on to Williams. I wonder just where *does* she live? What a coincidence it might be if she lives near me. But when she turns off Williams onto Centennial Avenue, and again on Raymond, I realize she's not exactly a neighbor, but certainly in my neighborhood.

Set way back from the street, her home looks like a surviving out-building, maybe it had been for gardening when another, larger home stood in front. Could the original house have been torn down, or was this the original home simply set so far back from the street?

With the front expanse of the house covered with nine side-by-side windows. The front entrance is on the side, facing the next home to the right. Not being able to see the door makes the home look even more like an extra building-turned-livable cottage.

Once we are inside, I can tell the historic home has been nicely remodeled and could be super cute— except when she moved in, she never unpacked. Boxes, stacked two and three high, are everywhere. Her furniture looks as though it was carried through the front door and set wherever. Although I see writing on the boxes, there is no rhyme or reason to what is where or which room. A bedframe leans against a mattress which leans against the wall that probably is the dining area. A fifty-inch flat screen TV leans against a low cabinet, probably to set the TV on, in what probably is the living room.

There is, however, a path between the boxes and furniture toward a door near the kitchen. It looks like a pantry door, but when Abbie leads me to it, she turns with an apologetic expression. "This is where I actually live."

She opens the door, flips on the light, and descends the stairs. I follow. The small, maybe four-hundred square foot basement has a computer desk with a raised shelf where two large computer screens are positioned to face the executive mesh chair that is pushed back from the desk. A CPU is tucked away in a side vertical compartment, and a large printer is inside a cabinet on the left side of the desk. There is a long-armed lamp, a light ring for holding a cell phone while posting or recording videos, and two rows of shelves that hold binders nicely marked by dates.

Nope, not a basement to declutter! The entire upstairs is another story. Ironically, here, in the basement, she is extremely organized. Upstairs, she never really moved in. Where does she sleep? I pivot to see what else is in the small space.

There is a comfy-looking recliner with a Yu-Gi-Oh fleece blanket draped on the armrest. "Ah, you sleep in the recliner?"

"Yes." She blushes. "I haven't set up my bed upstairs."

I nod slowly, considering where to begin. "Okay. Let me take pictures, you know, for my before, and I'll work up an estimate. Do you think everything upstairs is what you want to keep, or will there be some culling involved when we get you unpacked?"

"I have no idea. My friends packed everything for me because I was too overwhelmed when I bought this house. I was slammed up against a deadline for a customer's website. My friends offered and I let them. There could be anything in those boxes upstairs, including trash or dirty laundry, for all I know.

"Speaking of which, where are your clothes?" I pivot again, wondering if she is living out of a suitcase?

She moves to a door I hadn't notice and opens it. Ah, a closet… crammed full of shirts on hangers and a dresser below with four drawers.

"I see." I say in awe. "You've made it work."

She shrugs. "I had to have access to my clothes." She sighs. "I'm a mess."

"But you're very organized in this space… and online." I try to be positive where and when I can.

"So it appears." She purses her lips.

I smile. "I find that when your space is cluttered, you feel cluttered. Once we get your upstairs in order, you'll feel more like you are in order." I touch her shoulder and give a gentle squeeze. "Okay, I'll take pictures and call you when I have an estimate. We can get back together when you want and go over my thoughts."

"Yes. That would be great." She sits in her computer chair as if it is her only safe place. I smile and return to upstairs.

"What a cute place." I state to no one, since she stayed down in her lair.

Geniuses are funny creatures. The fact that my house was move-in ready when I came to Deadwood, it looks like a weekend rental complete with weekly cleaning service. It is no reflection of my ability to move and set up my own space. But when it comes to organizing other people's space, I'm a fully-functional master of the trade. As I snap pics on my phone, I make a mental note of framed wall hangings and furniture that I see and how it will look once we sort through all the boxes. She has everything needed to make this place look great. She just needs someone to inspire her to get it done. I consider who I could call for some muscle help, too. We are going to have some heavy lifting ahead of us.

Would Blaze be willing to help? Or any of his buddies? I'll have to ask. Assuming he's even talking to me anymore, after abandoning him with the Mister-and-Missus-Holmes debacle.

Chapter Five

"Hello?" I poke my head around the door before I enter my home. I have no idea what to expect. Will Frank and Mrs. Holmes be inside discussing the fact that they no longer own this home? Will Blaze be refereeing a verbal tussle? Will they turn on me the minute I enter and accuse me of squatting in their property? Or will they have made up and be doing the wild thing on my couch? Oh God, I do not want to see that!

Barkley greets me, peeking around the half-opened door, wags his tail like a water sprinkler set on high, and gives me an I'm-glad-you're-back buff. I pat his head.

"Are they gone, boy?" I ask quietly in case they are not. But with a quick scan I see Barkley and I are alone. I sigh with relief. "Whew!"

I need to get to working on Abbie's estimate, but I also need to fulfill my promise to Blaze. Should I put on something slinky and grab a bottle of wine before I head over to his house? What if Frank and Millie are there? Blaze has taken Frank to his house to wait out Mrs. Holmes's temper before. Would he take both of them over there to resolve this issue?

Why is Millie asking Frank's forgiveness this time? Is that really why she is here? If I were to show up dressed all sexy and with a wine bottle in hand and discover the two of them are still at odds with each other, that would be embarrassing. Inappropriate, too.

All these times that Frank sought refuge here in Deadwood, has she ever followed him to beg for his mercy? Frank never mentioned her coming after him. Only that he had to wait until she would allow him back into their home in Dallas. She seemed pretty determined before to punish him for losing at cards.

I sigh. "Barkley, what would you do?"

He barks.

"Yeah, I'd love to bark at them, too." I giggle. I cannot ring Blaze's doorbell and offer my gratitude for getting rid of them if they are standing right there. I walk over to the door in my kitchen leading to the balcony where I can see Blaze's house best. I don't see Frank's red Jeep anywhere. Where had Frank parked it? I didn't even notice the red Jeep when I fled to meet Abbie. He usually parks in my driveway or Blaze's. Is that a sign that they are gone?

I cannot confirm if Blaze is alone or not, but his lights are on and a shadow passes in front of the patio door. Is it Blaze? From this angle above Blaze's home, I can't tell if the shadow was as tall as him or shorter like Frank. I know for a fact it was not Mrs. Holmes. Her shadow would have more girth.

Barkley barks.

"What?" I ask him. Did he see something I didn't?

He walks around the island then rushes back to me with his food bowl in his mouth. He tosses it in the air and lets it land on the tile floor with a loud, hard-plastic bang. Then he picks it back up and tosses it closer to my feet.

I laugh.

"Okay, first things first." I tell him as I take the bowl and fill it with his food. His tail wags so hard his backend sashays with it. He pants his approval as I set the filled bowl where it was. My dog digs in as if he was starving. Which I know he's not, he ate just this morning. I too feel hungry. My summer salad from the late-lunch meeting with Abbie has digested and left me feeling the need for a bowl of something also. I look in my freezer for something quick and easy to heat up. A steamers bowl of chicken and pasta looks good enough and I pop it into the microwave.

I glance at the window overlooking Blaze's property. I long to go to him and sink into his embrace. I'm so curious about what is going on with the Holmeses and want to make good on that promise to make it up to him for abandoning them in the heat of the battle, between the sheets, as my junior high school self used to say when we read the note inside our fortune cookie. I sigh.

The microwave dings and I gingerly set my meal on the island counter. Putting my phone and laptop next to the plastic bowl, I dump the sauce over the meat and pasta, give it a stir, and open my computer to a blank spreadsheet template that will allow me to draw up an estimate for Abbie.

I chew and review the pics I took earlier. Two bedrooms, one bathroom, a living room, and kitchen-dining area combo; many, many boxes to unpack. How much of the contents of those boxes will be culled is an unknown variable. I laugh at my thought. I'm speaking to myself in programmers' language. Being around Abbie had brought back memories of programming classes I took in college.

```
>Begin
        >If x = keep, then
        >    x: = find location in house;
        >end
        >else
        >If x = donate, then
        >    x: = rebox for transport;
        >end
        >else
        >If x = trash, then
        >    x: = throw away;
        >end
        >print x.
        >end.
```

I laugh at myself for tapping into those memories from so long ago! Thank God I don't do that for a living! Helping people get organized and decluttering their space is so much more fun and rewarding, and less solitary. Abbie's tiny basement space flashes in my mind. How many hours a day does she sit there and stare at the computer screen?

"But I need you!" I hear a high-pitched, goose-like sound next door. It has to be Mrs. Holmes, aka Miss Prissy from the cartoon. I turn my gaze to the door that gives me access to the balcony overlooking Blaze's house. Should I? It's none of my business, but golly, I'm curious!

"Since when, Millie?" Frank's baritone voice bellows back.

"Let's go back inside and figure this out." Blaze's calm-cop voice follows the overly excited quarreling voices.

Now, I have to look. I walk over to the window, standing just out of their sight but where I can see them. Blaze has his hand on the couple's shoulders and is guiding them back into his house. Apparently, and thankfully, Frank has dressed. He no longer sports only a beach towel. Did he have his clothes at my house, intending to stay in my guest bedroom as usual?

Poor Blaze. What a hairy-pickle of a mess I left him with. Guilt swamps my gut. I really need to go over there and see what I can do to help.

Barkley barks.

Is he telling me he agrees? I grab his leash and head downstairs. Barkley wags his tail as we descend. Does he think we are going over for some play time or hot tub therapy? How I wish! We glide down the stairs, both of us panting when we reach the bottom and head toward Blaze's yard. Everyone has gone back inside his house, so I go straight to his front door and ring the bell. Barkley barks. I giggle at my dog's insistence for me to just walk in.

It's obvious he loves Blaze. I think I do, too.

"He'll hear the doorbell, Boo, be patient." I say with a chuckle. It's no wonder this dog chose me, we are two beans in one shell. The door opens and an exasperated Blaze stands before me. His expression morphs from an irritated, "What the—" to a relieved, "Thank God you're here," appearance. He reaches out and pulls me in by the shoulders, drawing Barkley along with me by his leash. I stumble into his foyer while Barkley glides in and obediently sits beside me without my saying a word. Frank and Mrs. Holmes are in the kitchen, silently staring at us, but I can tell they were in the middle of a heated discussion.

"I'm sorry to interrupt." I blurt out. I'm not sorry, but it seems like the thing to say. Frank closes his eyes and hangs his head. What has Mrs. Holmes badgered him about this time? Having reconciled myself to befriend Frank and coming to terms with allowing him to stay in my guest bedroom whenever Mrs. Holmes refuses to let him go home, I feel protective of him. "What's wrong?"

"Millie wants me to come home," Frank states. His eyes flit from me to Blaze, then to Mrs. Holmes.

She holds her chin high, as if she were facing a firing squad. "I love you, Frank. It's as simple as that."

Why is Frank not overjoyed she is here and wants him back home? What is going on? With her words of amore, I would expect the two of them to be cuddling and happily planning to leave. Wait! How *did* he get here? "Frank?" I consider my question carefully. "Where's your Jeep?"

His head sags forward as if the puppeteer cut the string that held his head up straight. "I lost it in a game."

Mrs. Holmes's eyes widen and her lips purse into a taut, straight line. She stammers and sputters like an old car firing on two cylinders. Then she shocks all of us. "It's alright, darling." She seems to be chewing her words before spitting them out. "I forgive you."

Blaze and I both jerk our heads in awe. I know for a fact that when Frank loses a poker game, especially when he loses something rather expensive, she is not so forgiving. I have sat up with Frank more than twice the last couple of months that I have lived next door, listening to his sad tale about his wife's intolerance to his gambling, especially his losing.

I get that. When momma and I learned that Daddy lost that one fateful game, we were stunned, but then when he committed suicide, we were devastated. It was the worst several weeks of my life. Not only because we found out that he had put up everything we held dear: our house, our car, even the furniture inside; in order to stay in the game. He desperately fought for a chance to win back what he had lost.

I lost my daddy, Momma lost her husband, we lost our way of living, and nearly became homeless.

I glance at Blaze and see the same confusion in his face. Who is this woman, and what has she done with the real Mildred Holmes? I think Frank is right, she's not telling him everything.

But is it really my business to drag it out of her? I admit, I have grown a soft spot in my heart for Frank, but in the end, this is between a husband and a wife.

I remain dumbfounded.

Blaze closes his gaping mouth with a pop. "Millie, I've never heard you speak so agreeably about Frank's gambling. It's always been a point of contention between you two." He tilts his head. His face turns stone-cold serious, like he's gone into interrogation mode. "Can you explain to me why you're not upset this time?"

Frank lifts his face to look at his wife. Her eyes bounce all over the place as if she were up against a rock wall, facing a pack of wolves. She can't seem to settle on one thing to look at. Her mouth opens and closes as if she were gulping air, then she mumbles, "Well, I—" She shakes her head. "I, uh." Her eyes land on Frank. "I love you, Frank. I want you home… with me."

I take a step toward her. Years of playing poker has made me an excellent reader of people's faces. She's lying through her cherry-red lipstick. "I call bull-turd."

Mrs. Holmes's face snaps toward me, her eyes narrow, but she remains silent.

"You're bluffing." I state matter-of-factly. "I know lying eyes when I see them. What are you hiding from Frank?"

Frank crosses his arms over his chest and looks down at her, this time shame has fled from his expression. "What is it, Millie?"

"Oh, Frank." She says in a flirty, less goose-like tone. "It's just that…" She swallows. "I have good news and bad news, darling. I just wanted to be able to tell you in private, when we got back home."

"What are you talking about?" Frank presses.

Blaze, Barkley, and I hold our positions. Should any one of us move, she might balk and go back to hiding the truth.

"Oh, alright." She glances at the three of us. "An attorney called. Your uncle Titus passed away."

Frank's head flops to the side. Was he deciphering if this was indeed the truth or more lies? "The man was eighty-nine years old, I'm not surprised he died."

His eyes narrow on her. "Is that your good news or bad?"

When she didn't answer, he pressed in. "What's that got to do with anything?"

I'm thinking Frank is right. Why would she run to Deadwood, begging him to forgive her foul temper, just to tell him that his uncle died. Wait! I know what's going on! I take another step closer to the kitchen and the couple. "Is there an inheritance?"

Mrs. Holmes snaps her gaze toward me and glares a hateful look as if I had just slapped the cards she was holding against her chest and exposed everything she was hiding.

"There is, isn't there? You're here because Frank has an inheritance, and you cannot receive it without Frank being present to… to sign paperwork… or something." I cross my arms challenging her even more. "Tell me I'm wrong!"

Her glare intensifies.

Barkley growls. I pat his head, "It's okay, boy." I assure my dog with a quiet, low voice, hoping I'm right. If Mrs. Holmes lunges at me, will Barkley attack back?

Now I understand why Frank wasn't overjoyed when she came at him with such public affection. He might not always be successful at poker, but he sure knew how to read his wife.

I have a newfound respect for my friend, Frank. He is not the sniveling, cowardly, wife-whipped husband I thought he was.

Eventually, she relaxes with the appearance of utter surrender. She sighs heavily. "You're not wrong."

Chapter Six

I wanted to jump up, swing my fist through the air, and yell, "Yeah!" But instead, I simply step back to where Blaze has stood this whole time and let Frank have a conversation with his wife.

Was greed the primary reason she threw Frank out when he lost at poker, and the reason she flew from Dallas, Texas to Rapid City, South Dakota, and then took a taxi to my house, (well, Kate drove her) trying so desperately to find him? Was greed the only reason she is so willing to beg him to come home? What a sad marriage they must have.

"Poor Frank," I think for the bazillionth time.

"Well, I have work to do," I say to Blaze more than Frank or Mrs. Holmes, dismissing myself from the awkward situation. "Come on Barkley, let's go home." I inch my way to the door.

"No, wait." Mrs. Holmes holds up her hand with long, red polished nails, like an out-of-place cross-guard for the school intersection. She turns back to Frank. Did she want us to witness what she was about to say?

"How did you get here?" She focuses on Frank.

He squirms under her fiery gaze. "I caught a ride."

"From whom?" She cocks her hip out to one side and slams a fist onto the shelf her position makes.

"A friend." His sheepish tone reveals more than I think he meant to.

"Franklin Dwayne Holmes." She enunciates each syllable of his name. "Are you having an affair here in Deadwood?"

"No." He said too quickly.

Was he? I run that conversation through my head. "…in Deadwood." She said "in Deadwood." Is he having an affair… just not in Deadwood? Oh, Frank, you sly dog. I look down at Barkley whose tongue is lolled over his open maw, he pants heavily as if he just ran up our stairs to the front door. I lift my eyes to Blaze. The detective looks as though he has figured out the same thing I have. We both keep our thoughts to ourselves. It's none of our business. Except Frank and Mrs. Holmes seem to keep dragging us into the middle of their marital problem. I huff to myself.

"I've gotta go." I blurt. "Barkley, come." I say to my dog and take a tighter hold of his leash to guide him with me out the door. We hurry to our house, where crazy chaos is not visiting at the moment.

My phone is ringing from inside the house when I reach the top of the stairs. Panting, Barkley and I enter. I rush to my cell phone laying beside my computer where I had walked away from my work. "Hello!" I wheeze.

Silence. I look at the screen. The caller is gone. I took too long. Thumbing my phone icon, I gasp when I see who has called me. "Huh? What did he want?"

I redial the number.

The man answers on the first ring. "Maribeth?"

"Yeah," I say. The sound of Big Mike's voice worries me. "You alright?"

"Sure." He answers. My gut tightens. Is he calling to tell me what a lousy person I am for bringing Uncle Donald to his underground lair and then sitting through Blaze's team's invasion?

"Look," I start to apologize before he chews me out. "I, uh..." My words are so feeble, empty, I cannot continue.

"Maribeth!" Big Mike repeats. "We need to talk."

He's whispering now. I gulp a knot of fear and dread. Was someone threatening Big Mike again? "Okay? When?"

"Now."

Barkley looks at me with kind puppy-dog eyes. He pants loudly while waiting for me to get off the phone and spend time with him. But now I have been summoned to Deadwood Tobacco Company's shop by Big Mike. Oh Lord, this can't be good. I quickly shove some biscuit treats into a hard rubber kong for Barkley's entertainment while I'm gone, grab my backpack purse, and rush outside.

"Sorry, boy." I say over my shoulder as I close the door behind me. Minutes later, I parallel park and turn off Kiley's souped-up engine. She sounds like a throaty sports car since Chris Fosdick gave her a makeover. I stand next to her, but I can't seem to go any further. My feet feel nailed to the street. I dread going inside the tobacco shop so much. Why was Big Mike whispering? Who else is in there with him? Was he in danger? Should I have run over to Blaze's and brought him along too?

"I'm so sorry. I am so, so sorry, guys," I practice as I manage to force my feet to move. This is worse than when I was in trouble and momma would tell me to go to my room and wait for her. Ugh! I square my shoulders and lift my chin. *I can do this.*

I walk in.

"Oh, thank God! There she is!" Randall hollers from what looks like a pacing routine that had only ended when I walked in. Where is everyone else? Are we alone? Oh, God! What has happened to Big Mike? Randall grabs my arm and drags me to the back of the store, where we zip out into the alley. I visualize a firing squad out here, taking aim for when I walk out. Are these my last seconds on this earth?

The co-owners of the tobacco shop are gathered around a torn and tattered box. Allen looks up. I can now see that the top where it should be taped down is hanging from the sides as if someone has torn the box while pulling on the flaps, or to pull it away from another person. I scan the guys. There are so many questions I want to ask.

"Maribeth!" Allen declares. "Didn't you say that if we find something that needs to be thrown away, just throw it away!"

"I, uh…" I shake the cobwebs in my head to loosen my tangled thoughts. This is so different from what I was expecting when I walked out here. I think I understand what is really happening. They are not about to kill me. They are squabbling over the declutter sorting. "What's going on?"

Randall marches past me, like the kid who tattletales in second grade. He turns to present his co-partners. "Allen, here, thinks everything from the basement is trash!" Randall put his hands on his hips and gyrates in an over-acting imitation of what Allen might have said before I was summoned. "If it wasn't trash, we wouldn't have dumped it in the basement!" He straightens, coming out of character and being himself. "But I keep telling him there could be hidden treasures down there and we have to go through everything to be sure. Huh?

Maribeth? Isn't that what you said when we first started down there?"

"Well, I… I believe I said we never know what we might find…" I swallow. "I also recall saying to separate the things from the basement into three categories, and *then* we can *verify* what is trash and what is treasure." I channel my inner second-grade teacher and attempt to take control of this squabble. Should I grab Randall and Allen by the ears and drag them to opposite corners where they will need to sit and think about their behavior toward one another?

"Now, Randall, why are you preventing Allen from sorting the items?" I ask.

"Because." Randall begins louder than before. "He is—"

I wave my hands in a downward motion, gesturing for Randall to lower his voice.

"He is not sorting things." Randall dials down his volume as he speaks. "He's just piling everything on the trash tarp, box and all. He doesn't even look through it."

"Okay. I walk over to the three tarps where two are holding a few items, and one is really overflowing with unopened boxes. "Yes, well. We should open each box and verify there isn't anything inside that is… of value." I hoped by using that particular word, I would be able to motivate Allen to look through everything.

Reluctantly and with a slight growl, Allen concedes to opening everything before sorting.

I turn to Randall. "There. Problem solved."

"For now." Randall grumbles.

"Yes, for now." I suppose I shouldn't have left these men to themselves to sort through all the stuff downstairs. But it hadn't been my idea to leave. Once I saw Mrs. Holmes and Kate standing at the entrance to the store and was accused of having an affair with Frank, I had to take care of that matter.

"Could I have a bottle of water?" I ask Wild William who is standing at the door to the alley with an ornery grin on his face. I turn to the other two, roll up my imaginary sleeves, and grab a box knife. "Let's get these boxes open."

I cut through the clear tape that had been used to seal them shut and shove the box aside. I cut the next one open. Looking up at Allen and Randall, who seem to be playing a game of freeze tag and they had recently been touched by the one who was *it*. "Come on. I did my part, now you do yours. Look through the contents of those boxes."

They jumped as if they had snapped out of their shock, and each took a box to sort through. By nightfall we had everything sorted. "Good." I say. "Let's take all the 'keep' things into the shop just in case it rains, or somebody wanders down here and thinks this is for free-pickings. Allen, you put all the trash things in the dumpster, and Randall, you take the second tarp and box up the items by categories for donating. We'll take it to wherever you want tomorrow." I turn to Allen.

He looks worried. "Where am I supposed to put the 'keep' items?"

I sigh. "Put them back in the basement for tonight. I'll come over in the morning and we will find a place for each item or re-determine if it truly is a 'keep' item."

He nods and begins hauling the things back to the front basement area.

I glance at the green door where I first was instructed to go when I asked to attend an underground high-stakes game. We had spoken in code about a karaoke game, but we really were talking about a poker game.

I purse my lips, feeling nostalgic. Behind that door lay the solutions to all my money problems, and yet the greatest risk to my soul, my sanity, and possibly even my life. I feel sad, too, that the games have been halted by Blaze and his team of detectives. But when I really think about it, if Uncle Donald had taken over, the way he had planned to, these games wouldn't have been the same. He ran his games with a sleight of hand. No one realized the amount of control he had over the outcome of the games. It would never be the same for me here in Deadwood. If I were honest, it was the risk that gave it the thrill and made the game what it was. There was nothing else in life that felt like that.

I return to the tobacco shop and find Big Mike behind the bar, serving drinks to customers who were also lighting up cigars and chatting. I lean on the polished wooden surface. "Listen," I exhale and wait for him to approach me. "I want to apologize for bringing Don—"

Mike waves me off with a white bar towel in his hand. "Nah! It weren't none of your doings." He wipes the bar in front of where he stands. "Truth be told, you bringing that pompous ass here saved *me* from going to jail." He lifted his eyes to me. "I mean, if that jackass from Denver hadn't come in here throwing his weight around and telling me how he was taking over my business, I would have been the one going to prison. As it was, I could raise my hands in surrender and say, 'Officer, I'm not the man you're looking for.'" Mike laughs. "I was like: Mister Donald Conway, there is the new boss, you need to speak to him about hosting this here game." Mike concluded with a slap on the bar and a hooting, belly laugh. "You bringing Conway in here was the best thing you could have done to save my bacon that night, and I appreciate ya for it."

I stared at Big Mike for a long moment. "You mean… you're not mad at me?"

"Mad? At you? Nah! You're the best player I ever seen."

His words stick in my craw like a corncob gone down sideways. I wasn't the success he thought I was. It was all a hoax, a magician's sleight of hand. Uncle Donald had seen to it that I won, and he took a portion of my winnings. Without me even suspecting. How could I have been so stupid? So naïve?

"You're what we like to call a draw." Mike continues. "Them other players hope you'll be here. They get their tail feathers all spread out and want to prove they got what it takes to beat ya." His eyes smiled along with his mouth exposing the one gold tooth. "You're good for business."

I nod. I'm too choked up to say anything. If only he knew the truth about my ability to win all the time. He hands me an ice water with a lemon. "Here, on the house."

He winks at me. It's a joke because water if free anyway, but still a kind gesture. I sip the water and feel grateful for friends, even though they have no idea what a fake I am.

Chapter Seven

"I hate to ask," I say, even though I don't really mean it. I have to ask. I need some strong men to move Abbie's furniture while she and I empty boxes and find a place for everything. I am at his door, prepared to beg if I have to.

My plan for her is to designate a location and put it there. If she is unsure, then sort it into one of two categories: give away or trash.

My grandma Lizzie always said, "A place for everything and everything in its place." It's an excellent motto when organizing peoples' stuff, too. "Thank you, Grandma Lizzie," I say to myself as I glance heavenward.

It's not like I know a lot of strong men, except Blaze… and the young salesman at the tobacco shop. But I don't feel I know Ian well enough to ask him for physical labor. He and his bosses are clients of mine. I don't think it's good etiquette to ask a client for a favor. With the exception of Abbie. She and I have worked out a barter for our services. I am helping her declutter her home and she is helping me design a website that will help me have the most potential to draw in new clients.

Besides, any excuse I can come up with to spend time with Blaze is a bonus to me. Asking for his help is just as good of an excuse as asking to borrow a cup of sugar.

I smile, thinking how he came to my house when Frank showed up out of nowhere. Blaze's instincts for trouble flared and he came knocking on my door asking for a cup of sugar as a guise to see if I was alright. I wasn't. Frank had scared the bejeezies out of me. It is still a puzzle to me why Mrs. Holmes has gone to so much trouble to chase after Frank this go round.

Since Blaze and I haven't developed our *lover's radar-telepathy* yet, I am here on his porch to verbally ask for help. "I hate to take you away from your leisure time… on your day off… I mean, if you were planning to mow or something…of course you weren't, you'd have been up at five o'clock to mow, so I don't know what you had planned today…"

Why can't I just say it?

He shifts to his other foot, filling his door frame with the broad shoulders I enjoy snuggling into, obviously displeased with my hem-hawing around. His eyebrows draw together. "Just ask."

I look up into his tempestuous eyes. I love those dark stormy green eyes, even when I'm worried about intruding into his personal time. I sigh. "I need you and hopefully some of your buddies to help a client of mine move furniture."

"Move furniture? You want to borrow my truck?"

"Oh, no." I laugh, stupidly exposing my nervousness. "It's already in her house, we just need to move it into its proper location and maybe some assembly will be required…"

He steps back into his foyer. "You want some coffee?"

I tilt my head in confusion. "Sure."

Why did he ask me that? Was that his way of saying he will help? I follow him into the kitchen. He pours two cups and hands me one. "When do you need this help?"

Okay, we are back on subject. "Well, today, if possible. Do you know anybody who would be free today… to help?"

He smiles and sips his coffee. "Yeah, I know some guys."

He tilts his head toward Frank who is on the back deck with Millie. They seem to be engrossed in a conversation.

Why does Blaze look so… mischievous?

I mirror his smile. "Okay… so… why do you look like you know something I don't?"

"Do I?"

"Yes, you do." I sip my coffee. I love his coffee. I don't know what he does different from me but his coffee tastes richer and yet smoother than mine.

"I don't know anything you don't, or do I?" He waggles his eyebrows.

I tilt my head the other way. What did that mean? "Okay…so… we've got Frank. Can you give one or two more friends a call, or…"

"Yeah, I'll call them." His ornery grin widens.

"What?" I look down at my clothes. Is my fly unzipped, is one of my boobs sticking out? What?

"I was just wondering." His eyes smolder with desire. I love that look on him.

"Wondering what?" I ask, my knees turning to pudding.

"What's in it for me and my buddies."

"Oh." I snap out of my lust-filled fantasy. I honestly hadn't thought he'd want to be compensated. I was hoping for a friends-helping-friends sort of thing. "What do you all expect? Money? Beer and a pizza? A referral?"

He laughs and steps toward me, setting his coffee mug on the counter. He takes me into his arms. I struggle to keep from spilling my coffee.

"Well, for one thing, it will give Frank an excuse to get away from Millie for a while." He glances at the poor man who looks like he's shrinking into the patio chair while Millie seems to be growing larger, looming over him. "How about we give Frank and my buddies beer and pizza, and you and I come back over here and" —his brow leaps high on his forehead— "you thank me in person."

"Ooooh." I say in a as sultry of a tone as I can muster this early in the morning. "Will that be reward enough, Mister Hemingway?" I blink coyly and duck my chin close to my collar bone.

"Weellll," he chuckles. "After moving and assembling furniture I might need some hot tub therapy like Barkley. Perhaps we can start there and see where the night goes."

My eyebrows bob flirtatiously. "That sounds like a good start. So… I can bring Barkley, too?"

"Of course." He cups the back of my head, lacing his fingers into my hair, and draws me closer to his face. Gently, he places a soft kiss on my lips. I close my eyes and wrap my arms around his neck. Not-so-gently, I pull him closer and our kiss intensifies, building in direct proportion to the thrill that courses through my soul when his body is so close to mine. I press into him, wanting more, but my lungs burn for oxygen.

I pull back, gasping for breath. "I'm sorry, but we need to get your buddies assembled and go to Abbie's house by ten this morning." I cringe at the business-like tone in my voice. I really wanted to continue with what we were doing but duty calls.

He frowns. Lust burns in his eyes. "Aw, Honey… do we gotta?" There's a teasing tone in his voice. Then he laughs. "Okay. I'll give them a call."

Two hours later, we have gathered outside of Abbie's house. Blaze was able to get two of his detective buddies to come. I purse my lips when they arrive. Embarrassment filling my face with warmth. These are two of the three men Blaze had with him when they raided the poker game the other night. Will they think of me as a criminal?

I glance at Blaze. Suddenly, I'm having second thoughts about having Blaze and his buddies help us. He flashes me a smile. I wince an uncertain smile back. "These are your buddies who will come help the instant you call?" I ask.

His grin widens. "Yep."

They look strong enough to me. I'm certain they can do the job. Certainly more than Frank. He looks fit and healthy, but not... body builder form like the detectives. It feels so awkward having these same guys here— along with the extremely large white elephant that stands just behind me.

Frank's phone chimes. He excuses himself and walks away from the rest of us. It's Millie. I can tell by the way Frank begins speaking in a hushed, wimpy tone.

Blaze turns away from watching Frank walk off and introduces Joe Scott and Matt Cleburne to me. At the poker raid, there were no introductions. We give each other knowing but polite nods, then I introduce the three of them to Abbie, who seems oblivious to the tension between us. She's so happy to have help getting her house in order she would not notice if the gigantic white elephant started lifting poles with its trunk and setting up tents in her yard while juggling a dozen colorful balls in the air.

"Look, fellas." I figure I'll just clear the air and send Miss White Elephant on her merry way. "I, uh, want to expla—"

"It's okay, Maribeth." Joe chuckles. There's a twinkle in his eye. "Blaze explained the whole thing. We get it."

Matt slaps Blaze on the back. "Yeah, it's cool. We're so glad to see Blaze with a woman in his life, we don't care what your background check reveals."

Blaze's cheeks darken.

Background check? Did Blaze run a background check on me? I open my mouth to ask, but Blaze beats me to the punch.

"Stop it." He says to them, then turns to me. "They're kidding, I swear." He shoots a glaring look toward the guys.

But I don't know if they are kidding or not.

Frank returns to us, shoving his phone in his back pocket. Blaze speaks to me, but his eyes are on his buddies. "But they do know about Conway and how he, uh," Blaze glanced at Abbie. "How he tricked you."

He claps his hands and rubs them vigorously. "Let's get this party started. Where do you want us to start?"

Frank's phone rings. He steps away, speaking quietly into the device. I'm not sure how much help he is going to be with Millie calling him every five minutes.

I sigh. I don't feel relieved at all, but at least I know they are not holding what they know about me against me. Are they? No, surely not. Why would they agree to come help if they were? I feel wary of their presence, like I should be careful what I say and do. I look deeply into Blaze's eyes. I can trust him, right?

"Okay." I hesitate. I don't have any other choice. If I'm really honest with myself, Abbie and I can't do this by ourselves. Well, we could, but, my goodness, it would take much longer and we would be completely worn out. Maybe I should have asked the girls to help us instead. Michelle, Cindy, Suzie and Tricia would have voluntarily come to help, but they would only be available on the weekend. If I want to get this done today, these men are my best option. I just hope it doesn't come back to bite me on the… *derrière* later.

"Abbie and I will work on the boxes and as we get them out of your way," I begin. Frank returns and listens with the other men. "We'll ask you guys to move furniture into place and/or assemble stuff, like bed frames. I have a small toolbox in the trunk of Kil—" I swallow. "my car, when you need them. Okay?"

"Yep." Joe says with a jerk of his head.

Matt nods, too.

We enter Abbie's house and get to work. Frank's phone rings every five minutes. Millie will not leave him alone! So much for him getting away from her for a while.

Abbie moves boxes away from the furniture so the guys can get started. She has the boxes marked by room, which helps a great deal for sorting. The kitchen seems the best place to start. I cut the tape and Abbie goes through the contents. We put her possessions away in an organized, functional manner according to proximity to where they will be used. The men take bed frames to the two bedrooms and are chatting while assembling them. We can hear their teasing jabber, and smile at one another. Frank keeps rushing from the room with the phone to his ear.

"Men!" We giggle and keep putting her things away.

"So," Abbie talks while she puts cups in the cabinet. "I'm thinking about putting a dynamic, rotating image gallery on your home page with before-and-after pictures. You do have permission to publicly display your previous customers' work, don't you."

"Yes, it's in their contract just like the one you signed."

"Great. So, I'm thinking we can make that your banner on your home page and then a section with your name and a link to contact info. Below that we could put some testimonials." She turns from reaching in the cabinet to smile at me. "What do you think?"

I hand her two more cups and return her smile. "I think… I love it."

"Good. I'll get that together tonight and show you tomorrow."

"Okay, great."

Joe's voice drifts from down the hall. "Denver, I guess."

I hear Blaze's voice. "Seriously? How do you know?"

My hearing turns like a satellite-seeking dish to listen.

"We don't actually. It's just an assumption." Matt adds to the conversation.

"You know what they say about assuming." Blaze states jokingly.

"You don't need any help being an ass, Hemingway." Joe says.

"Oh, yeah, it takes one to know one." Blaze jests. "But, seriously, do you have any idea where he went?"

"No. He walked out and disappeared in a black SUV. His bail bondsman was pretty peeved." Joe says.

"Yeah, I'd think so." Blaze replies. "It'll cost the courts a lot of money if he disappears."

"Are they calling a bounty hunter?" Matt asks.

"Not yet." Joe says.

"Hmm." Blaze replies.

My heart speeds up and my throat suddenly goes dry. I choke against the scratching sensation, coughing into my fist.

"You need water?" Abbie looks concerned and turns to pat me on the back.

I swallow hard, getting my cough under control. "Excuse me a minute."

I wander toward the voices down the little hall, bumping into Frank as he retreats to take yet another phone call, and lean against the door frame, listening.

Three sets of eyes turn toward me. "Who are you talking about?"

Blaze's Adam's apple bobs as he walks to me. Clasping my shoulders, he says, "Honey, Conway was released on bail."

Chapter Eight

"This looks great, guys." I compliment the boys at the tobacco shop. "Doesn't it feel better?"

"Indubitably." Wild William grins. His partners and I turn to look at him. He's never used such a high-dollar word before.

"Yes, indubitably." I agree by repeating his exact word, which I never use as well. I laugh with the guys as we look around at their accomplishment.

Their front basement is a well-organized storage space now, rather than a pile of boxes, furniture, and stuff. I take "after" pictures for Abbie to put on my new website and for my portfolio. I shake William's hand, then Randall's, then Allen's. I put out my hand to the salesclerk, Ian, but the sound of the front door chimes and he bumps my fist instead, and runs upstairs to see to the customer who just walked in.

William hands me a check for my services. "Here you go."

"Thanks." I tuck it in my backpack purse. "It was a pleasure working with you guys."

"You were great! I don't think any of us could have gotten that basement organized without your help, Maribeth." Allen says.

I smile. I can feel the heat filling my cheeks. It always feels good to have satisfied customers, and more photos to support my claims that I can organize anybody's space. I leave the basement feeling on top of my game.

"Say, Maribeth." Big Mike is standing behind the bar, wiping clear, high-ball glasses.

"Yeah?" I pause in front of him.

He looks around conspiratorially, then waves me closer to where he leans over the polished surface. "Listen, I'm not giving up on my side-gig, you know?"

I tilt my head. "Side? Gig?"

"Yeah, you know. The Karaoke Night gig." He winks at me.

I blink. "Oh." I swallow. "That."

When I first came here looking for a high-stakes game, Big Mike spoke to me in a cryptic code, calling the poker games Karaoke Night, until he knew he could trust me. He told me the Karaoke Night was at midnight, which meant the games began at midnight. He handed me a card that simply stated, "Green door." I put the puzzle together and found the green door in the alley and attended my first game that night.

Since the game was raided by the police, my boyfriend, Blaze, in the lead on the raid, I had hoped my temptation to solve any-and-all of my financial problems would be behind me. Now, Big Mike tells me he's not giving up. "What does that mean exactly?"

He grins as his wooly caterpillar eyebrows jumps in place. "You know."

"I'm not sure I do." I must be feverishly digging a hole and pulling the dirt over my head to say this. I know exactly what he means, I'm just hoping I've got it all wrong. I paste on my poker face, waiting for him to say it.

"Another underground gaming place." He straightens his spine. "You didn't think I would quit after your friend, Conway—"

"He is not my friend!" I pounce in the middle of his assuring me he would not give up hosting high-stakes games.

He nods, knowingly. "I misspoke. You don't think that Conway is the first of his kind to try to come into Deadwood and take over a good thing, do ya?" Big Mike picks up a cigar from the ash tray behind the bar and puffs on it a few times to revive the lit ash. "It just so happened that Conway made his attempt to take over on the same night that the police decided to try to shut us down. Conway conveniently availed himself to be the scapegoat." Mike puts his cigar down on the wide lip of the glass ash tray and goes back to wiping out glasses. "We'll find another place to hold the games." Looking directly into my eyes. "You're always invited."

I gulp back twin emotions, thrill and dread. "I can't."

"Why not?"

"I always thought I had a gift. Turns out, it was nothing more than a sleight of hand," I say. "Donald revealed to me that he controlled everything, like a puppeteer. Every time I played, I won, but only because he made sure it happened. Then he got a cut of my winnings. I had no idea this was happening behind my back." I drop my head. "I feel so… naïve."

Mike sets a clean glass down and turns his full attention on me. "That's not true for when you played here."

I stare at him. "What do you mean?"

He tsks his tongue. "Maribeth, Conway didn't show up here in Deadwood until the other night. You've been playing in our games off and on for the past several months, and you won every time. That's not a coincidence. You're good. Real good. Too good." A twinkle sparkles in his eyes. "Nobody is pulling puppet strings around here. Everything you did, you did on your own, using that brilliant brain of yours." He tapped my temple.

Heat fills my cheeks, and his words gently float into my brain. "You're right." I stare at nothing along the bar. "Donald wasn't here." I stand straighter. "That was all me."

Mike grins and lifts his cigar for another puff. He gives me a shrug nod, agreeing with me.

"But…" I continue my thought. "My daddy gambled, too. He was really good also, at least that's what he thought. Like me, he was being manipulated by Donald. When Daddy lost that one time— one time, Mike! He committed suicide."

Mike considered what I said, while wiping another glass. "Sounds to me like your dad had more of a reason to off himself," Mike jerks his eyes to mine. "I'm sorry, I didn't mean to be so insensitive. I'm so sorry for your loss," he adds.

I shrug.

"I'm just saying, maybe your dad and Conway had some sort of an agreement and when that one fateful game didn't turn out the way they intended, well, I'm thinking your dad owed Conway something he couldn't repay and that was why…"

I tilt my head. "You know, I was thinking some of the same thoughts as that. I really wonder what Daddy had gotten himself into that *one* loss would put him in a mental state as severe as carrying out suicide."

Mike shrugs. "It makes sense to me that there was more to it than just losing a game."

I nod, thoughtfully. "Thank you, Mike." I smile. "I appreciate you more than you know."

His face split with an ornery grin, "Oh, that's what all the good-looking women say."

I laugh and he chuckles.

"You're a good friend." I pat his hand as he pauses from wiping the counter with his bar rag.

"So are you, Maribeth."

I leave the tobacco shop feeling ten feet tall *and* on top of my game. While I still realize playing a high-stakes game of poker is risky, even though I'm good at it, there's still a chance I might not win. But at least now I know when I win, I win on my own merit, not because somebody like Donald is pulling the strings. Hopefully, when I lose, IF I lose, it won't cost me my sanity.

There was something else behind my dad's death besides his inability to accept the loss. This knowledge is so freeing. I'm still smiling when I get into Kiley and drive home.

Only one dark cloud hovers over my happy thoughts. What does Donald intend to do next? A shiver ripples down my spine. With Barkley in my house, I know I am safe from any intruders, such as Donald or his goons. If they come back to Deadwood to finish Donald's plans to branch out to the Black Hills, can Blaze protect me from the gangster-wannabe? I swallow hard and continue up the hill for home. I desperately need to snuggle with my dog.

But, as I drive down my street to where I can see my driveway. A red Ford F-150 pickup is parked there. This isn't Uncle Donald's style of vehicle. He goes for the ominous black SUV style with dark tinted windows. But could it be him anyway? Is he here incognito? Once again, I toy with the idea of driving by like I am not me. But if it is Donald, he knows Kiley and her souped-up body to accommodate her amazing new motor, very well. And the rumble as I drive by draws attention to the two of us, no matter who I am trying to avoid.

I cautiously pull into my driveway, but don't automatically open my garage door. I don't want to give whoever this is any advantage over me. The red pickup is parked on the side of the drive where I do not park Kiley. Someone either accidentally parked on that side, or they know me well enough to park out of my way when I come home.

Oh geesh! Who is this? Why did I not buy a gun?

The windows are tinted so dark I can only see a silhouette. The driver door opens. A shoe, then a pant leg emerges, followed by the man's body. It looks like…

No, it can't be. I don't believe it!

Chapter Nine

"Frank? What are you doing here?"

My phone rings. Much to my embarrassment, I jerk at the sound. Glancing quickly at my screen, I don't know the number. Frank opens his mouth, but I hold up a finger and answer my phone.

"This is Maribeth." In case this is a potential client calling from the amazing website Abbie designed and published, I use my professional voice.

"Hi." The person responds and rambles on about how they were looking through my new website and was impressed with my work… yada, yada, yada. Meanwhile Frank and I stare at each other. I make a face, apologizing for making him wait. He makes an equally non-verbal face and shrugs as if to say, "It's okay."

"I'd be happy to discuss this further." I say. "Let's schedule a meeting…" When do I have an opening? I lean into Kiley and get out my backpack purse. Inside I have an appointment calendar. I thumb over to next week, then the next. "Looks like I have time for an initial consult, next month." I give them the date and time.

"I know." I say empathetically when they complain about the wait. "But it's the soonest I have available."

They agree, and I write it down. "Can I reach you at this number?" I note the phone number displayed on my phone. "Okay. See you then." I say too quickly and hang up.

Lifting my eyes to Frank, I tilt my head. "What's going on, Frank?"

A grin is his reply. But I don't like it. What is he up to?

I walk closer. "Seriously, why are you here? I thought you and Millie worked things out?"

His dark, wiry brow shoots up toward the receding hairline that looks more like a shadow with his tight electric-razor trim. "I was hopeful when she came here trying to find me that she had changed," he says. "We bought this red truck in Rapid City and drove home together. I thought we were the old lovebirds we had been when we first got married. She certainly seemed that way." He grinned mischievously. "All the way home, she made me stop twice to get a hotel so we could—"

"I get it!" I stop him with a cross-guard palm. He dropped his arms to his side. Disappointment sagged his lips into a frown. Oh golly me. He was about to tell me every detail, with gestures to make himself clear. I didn't want to have to squirt bleach into my ears to wash that image from my brain. I didn't need to know any details about their renewed relationship other than they have made up. How they went about their sex life was their business and certainly not mine.

"Okay." I say. "So… why are you here?"

"She lied." His face drops forward like somebody just clobbered him in the back of the head.

"Frank?" I say, startled by his sudden about-face sentiment. Gosh, do I want to know what happened? Since I made a commitment to be Frank's friend, I feel obligated to ask. "What did she lie about?"

Slowly he lifts his watery, sad, bloodshot eyes. When had he begun to cry? "The only—" A hiccup escaped his throat. "R-reason she wanted me back so bad that she flew here to find me, was because she had made an appointment with that lawyer. You know, the one she said had called. The minute we got home, she changed clothes and told me to get in the pickup. I thought we were going to go have some more... adventures." He chose his words carefully this time. A smile quivered at his lips. "But she took us straight to the law office and we sat down to listen to what I had inherited."

I gawk at him. Millie only wanted him back for the inheritance. I knew it! How sad. But why would he be back here so soon, just because her heart was enamored with the money rather than him? I tilt my head.

"But, Frank, she's always been pretty..." How do I say this delicately. "Focused on your winnings and angry when you lost... why is this different."

He chuckled. "Because of what I inherited."

I lower my head so I can roll my eyes without Frank seeing me do it. I wish he'd just tell me what's going on. "What did you inherit?"

"Something Uncle Titus was very proud of."
A smile wavered on his lips as his throat constricted
with emotion. "I remember as a kid him showing
me his collection. Me and my cousins would go out
with him and help scour his place. He had some
land outside of a small suburb of Houston. To us
boys, we were finding all kinds of incredible stuff.
The Houston Archeological Society and Rice
University paid Uncle Titus to lead expeditions to
dig up more of the very things we boys found and
pocketed just cause we thought they were neat-o."

"What sort of things?" I ask. "Valuable
things?"

He looked deep into my eyes. "Valuable?
Yeah, they were valuable to my cousins and me, to
Uncle Titus. Those college boys were pretty excited
about it cause it showed evidence of the first
settlements in the area, but they weren't of any
value like you're thinking." He paused. His mouth
wrinkled into a half frown. "Wasn't as valuable as
Millie was thinking, either.

"What exactly did you receive from your
uncle?"

"Shadow boxes with items that we found
carefully placed on sheets of cotton, shards of
pottery, medicine bottles, wooden utensils, spoons

and such. Treasure boxes where we put jewelry and things too big for the shadow box— a bible even."

"Archeological stuff?" I ask.

"Yeah."

"Not diamonds or rubies?"

"No." He shook his head. "Costume jewelry, gold plated with glass stones that probably looked real pretty in its day."

"But nothing of real value?" I confirm.

"Well, it was valuable to Uncle Titus." His voice wavered as it grew in volume. "Those university boys thought it was real valuable! They got all kinds of excited and treated each piece like it was precious. And it was precious!"

"I know. I get it. I'm not saying it wasn't special. What I am asking you is this: was Millie so disappointed when she found out what you had inherited, that… she… I don't know, kicked you out… again?"

Frank's eyes watered. "No."

"No?" I was so expecting him to say yes, I couldn't believe my ears. "She didn't kick you out?"

"She sure did not." Frank puffed up like a peacock. "I left her!"

"Oh!" I stumbled backward. I never expected to hear this. "You left her?"

"I sure did. I told her she didn't love me for me." He shoved a thumb at his chest. "I told her, I was through being her sugar daddy—"

I stifled a giggle. "Frank, I don't—"

"I'm through giving and giving and giving. All she does is take, take, take. And then when Lady Luck gives me the finger, what did my loving wife do? She throws me out and I gotta drive all the way up here to South Dakota where the only place I have to live is… was available to me, with no questions asked."

A wave of guilt makes my neck shrink. I now own that refuge, and at first wouldn't let him stay here. Thank goodness, I got over myself on that issue. As an act of pay-it-forward, I agreed to allow Frank refuge whenever he needed it. But wait a minute…

"So… what are you thinking you're gonna do now? You moving to South Dakota?"

"Not only South Dakota, but Deadwood." His eyes twitch as his lips curl into a wicked smile.

I stare at him. Was he thinking he would move in here? We'd be housemates? Um, no. I stammered. "I, uh, don't think—"

"Oh, don't worry, Maribeth!" He waved my concern away, as if swiping his hand down through the air would slap my thoughts out of the space between us. "I'm not thinking I can live here with you. You won possession of this house fair and square. I'm gonna find me another place. All I ask, is that you let me bunk here for a while 'til I find another house."

"I, uh, I." Why can't I put two words together? Why can't I just say No! I hear myself say, "Sure."

What have I done! How could I agree to let Frank stay here until he buys another house? What was I thinking? My phone rings. I stammer to answer it. "H-hello?" I say more as a question than an answer.

"Miss Thorp?" The caller says.

I cringe for not answering more appropriately. "Yes, th-this is Maribeth Thorp." I reply while still staring at Frank. I can't shake the cobwebs that now tangle my mind. "How can I help you?"

The caller is female. She tells me her name, but my brain cannot absorb the information. She wants an initial consult for a declutter. I can't even remember what she said her space is. I need to be writing this down. I don't even know where I put my pen or notebook where I wrote the other caller's information. I stammer something about, "Can I call you back?"

She hesitates, then says, "Sure." And starts saying something else, but I hang up on her. Ah, if she lets me help her with a declutter, I'll be back in Lady Luck's good graces.

I put my phone away and turn to Frank. "So... what are you thinking? A couple of months at the most?"

He shrugs. "I have no idea."

Oh geesh! This can't be happening. I don't want Frank living with me long term. I've just taken on Barkley, a retired police dog with arthritis and therapy sessions. Blaze and I have just worked out the kinks for the possibility of a relationship. My personal organizer business is getting into gear. My calendar is quickly filling with clients. How can I possibly take on a housemate who is as needy as Frank?

How can I not?

Why doesn't Blaze swoop in here and save me from this? His instincts are usually fine-tuned to my needs. Why not now? I look at Frank. My eyes narrow. I can feel my spine hardening. I know what I need to say. Can I say it?

"Frank," I take a step toward him. "This plan of yours doesn't work for me."

His eyes widen. "Wha—" tears fill his eyes. "You're kicking me out, too?"

"I'm not kicking you out, Frank. You never lived here. As your friend I let you crash here once in a while when you needed to, but this is my house now. Not yours. If you want to move here to Deadwood, permanently, you need to stay in a hotel, or rent a place, until you find the house you want to buy. As a respectable business woman, I can't let you stay here for what will probably turn out to be months on end. Maybe even six to twelve months. Who knows how long it will take you to find a house and close on it." I shake my head. "I'm sorry... no I'm not sorry. I still consider you a friend, but I'm not your patsy. You can't take advantage of me like that. A friend would not take advantage of me like that."

I realize I'm breathing hard. I need to stop spewing words and start breathing. "You need to go." I step back.

Frank's puppy-dog eyes and pouty lip make my heart ache, but I stick to my conviction. I open my door and gesture for him to walk out. Slowly he takes a step and then another. As he passes me at the threshold, I prepare to close the door behind him. "Nice truck, by the way." I blurt out without thinking.

He turns back to me as if I just extended him a reprieve and indicated he could stay after all. I shake my head, reaffirming he has to keep going. He walks out to the deck and starts down the stairs.

"Be safe." I call out to him. Gaaaaah. I need to shut up and close my door. Barkley barks at me. He has a stiffer backbone than I do. But not today! I did good. I stood up to Frank and didn't let him run all over me. "Yay Me!"

I close the door and scratch Barkley's head. "What should we do for dinner?" I ask my dog.

My phone rings again. "Wow, clientele is really picking up." I say to Barkley as I lift my phone. I don't know the number, so I use my professional voice, "This is Maribeth Thorp."

Silence.

"Hello? How can I help you?"

"Maribeth."

My heart stops for a second or two. I can't breathe. No sound comes out of my gaping lips. close my eyes, gather myself, then speak.

"Uncle Donald? What do you want?"

Chapter Ten

"We need to talk." Donald says in a short and not-so-sweet voice that makes a hundred spiders crawl out of my hair and cascade all over my body.

"What about?" I choke. The child within is backing away to a nice, dark, safe corner where she can hide. The adult in me locks her knees and lifts her chin a notch and a half.

"About why your father committed suicide," he growls.

Because he lost a poker game where he had bet everything he owned and then lost his will to live along with his mind… right? That's what I thought happened. Have I been wrong all this time? Ah, I didn't really want to be wrong about that. Please don't tell me that's not how it really happened. I can't breathe. "Why *did* my father commit suicide?"

"That's why we need to talk," he snarls.

The blood surging against my ear drum is trumping with a high card for who can be the loudest: my heartbeat or Donald's voice.

"Well, go ahead… talk." I try to resume my spine-of-steel that I had used with Frank. It feels more like clay. Soft clay.

He laughs. "We need to talk in person."

"Where are you?"

"Ah, wouldn't you like to know?"

My temper is starting to make little bubbles. What kind of game is he playing now? If he wants to talk in person, don't I need an address? "What do you want, really, Mr. Conway?"

"Aw, now, no need for that, Maribeth. I'm asking for a civilized conversation between two colleagues."

The bubbles are growing bigger.

"Colleagues!" I spit when I speak. Scraping my teeth across my lips to retrieve the splattered saliva, I sigh deeply. I have to calm down. He can't get me rattled. This is nothing more than a game. I'm very good at games. I straighten to my full height, shake out my arms, and settle into a resting poker face. "Alright. What did you have in mind?"

"I'll let you know. Be available when I call."

The line goes dead. Was I next? The fire that was bringing my temper to a roiling boil dies. My temper deflates like a hot air balloon suddenly filled with cold air. My legs feel like the cartoon character Olive Oyl, all loose and floppy. Barkley leans against me, sensing my fearful emotions.

"I know boy." I rub my hand down his raised hackles. With a gulping swallow, I look out the window of my dining area toward Blaze's house. Should I place some duct tape in the window and direct a lamp light toward it? SOS. I press my fingers on my temples and close my eyes. "Blaze hear me, I need you. I'm about to die… maybe."

It felt good when I stood up to Frank. I wanted Blaze to swoop in and save me then, too, but I saved myself. This is different. Way different. Donald is not Frank. I cannot stand up to Donald and be confident that I will walk away safe… or walk away at all.

"God, I don't want to die." I mutter. "I just got my life together."

Donald gets what Donald wants. If he wants me dead, there's no clever counting of cards, or outwitting my opponent with an emotionless poker face that is going to protect me from whatever that man has in mind. I need help. I need Blaze's help. Not as a damsel in distress, but as a woman who is in too deep to climb up without someone sending down a lifeline.

I stagger out onto my deck, where I once watched, with great irritation, Blaze mowing my property at five AM. What a stupid thing to get angry about. The man was doing me a solid favor. Barkley joins me on the deck. He barks once, as if he were calling Blaze to come play with us.

A giggle effervesces from somewhere in my soul. Only this dog can make me snicker when I'm terrified out of my skin. I pat his head. "I don't think he can hear us, boy."

I lift my phone. My fingers tremble as I dial Blaze's number. Leaning on the railing, because I don't trust my legs. I watch his house as if the walls might turn invisible and I might see him when he answers.

"Hi, neighbor." Blaze's cheerful voice feels like warm water being poured over sore, achy muscles.

"Hi." I sigh.

"What's up?" He sounds wary.

"Oh, nothing much. Frank and Millie have split for good, apparently."

"No kidding?"

"Yeah. He came here, thinking he could move in until he found another house to buy."

"What! That could take months!"

"I know. That's why I told him he had to go stay at a motel or rent a place until he found the house he wants."

Barkley barks as if he is encouraging me to get to the heart of why I called.

Blaze laughs. "Tell Barkley hello."

"I will." I say while putting my hand on his soft furry head.

"So, good for you." Blaze continues.

"Yeah. Yay me." I say meekly.

"So… what's wrong."

I sigh. "Oh…" my eyes drop to Barkley who is patiently sitting beside me, panting. "Donald called."

"What?" Blaze's voice instantly changes. He loads his pistol with questions and starts firing. "Did he say where he was? What did he want? Why did he call you? Are you in trouble? Is he there at your house?"

"Whoa!" I giggle. "Slow down. No, I'm not sure, he wants to talk, maybe, no."

I can hear him swear under his breath. "I forgot my questions, to know what answers went with what?"

I giggle. "He didn't say where he is. I'm not a hundred percent sure what he wants. He says he wants to talk about why my father committed suicide. I may be in a lot of trouble. He is not at my house, thank God."

"You and your perfect memory." He chuckles. "Okay. So, we need a plan."

"Right." I breathe a sigh of relief. Blaze will know how to handle Donald.

As if he had been eavesdropping on every word Blaze said, Barkley barks. I scratch behind his ear. "Yeah, I hear ya, boy."

By the time I re-enter my house and lock the door behind me, Blaze walks through my front door. His cell phone is to his ear.

Barkley barks his greeting, "Hey, there!"

"Right. Okay." Blaze gives whoever is on the other end of his call my address. "Right, next door to me. Yes." He chuckles. "*That* house."

Oh, they are referring to my stairs. Everyone knows this house by the god-awful stairs to get to the front door. I rush to his arms and just inhale. He holds me with his free arm. The smell of his musk cologne and sun-kissed skin loosens my taut nerves. I lean my head back and look into his sea-green eyes. The emerald coast in Florida has nothing over Blaze's eyes when they are full of emotion. He disconnects and looks at me.

I purse a smile. "Thank you. I didn't know what else to do. This is the highest stakes game I've ever played in. Donald scares me. I don't know how to handle—"

"You were absolutely right to call me. Even if we weren't… you know… *seeing* each other, you would have been right to call the police for help."

Hold on… why the hesitation? Aren't we far enough along in our relationship to call each other boyfriend and girlfriend? Why can't he say we are dating? Or in a relationship?

Why do I care that he hesitated? My life could be on the line, and I'm worried about how Blaze interprets what we are developing together. Am I just a convenient booty call who happens to live next door?

What is wrong with me! This is *not* important right now! I shove the idiot thoughts behind me. Another time and place, we can address this issue. Focus! My mouth can't muster the slightest smile. I know I'm frowning, but I just cannot help it. I'm scared, and now I'm confused. Important or not, having my boyfriend hold me feels much safer than having my neighbor, who is a detective with the police, hold me with a half-hug while we figure out what to do about my life-and-death situation.

I step away from Blaze and wring my hands. He has gone into cop mode and I feel it. He is nothing more than the detective who will protect me from a bad and dangerous man, not my boyfriend who has warmed my bed, and couch, his bed, his couch, and other places.

"What are you thinking?" I ask.

He points at his cell phone. "I've called the team. You said Conway will call back. We are going to set up here, discreetly, and wait for that call. Once we know what he has in mind, we'll make some decisions about the best way to proceed."

"What if he doesn't call?" I hate the tremble in my voice and hands. "What if he just shows up."

"We don't think he will come here. For one, he left town when his bail bondsman specifically told him not to. Two, he knows I live next door, why would he risk being seen at your house?"

I snap. Glaring at Blaze. "Why would he leave town when his bail bondsman told him not to?" I lean toward him to make myself very clear. He has to understand this one thing. I continue, "Donald does what Donald wants to do. Nobody tells him what to do. Whether you're next door or living right here with me, nothing is going to stop him from doing what he wants to do. Even if I left and went somewhere else, he'd find me. He is used to being the big bossman…"

I can't stop rambling. My eyes widen. I feel like I'm drowning in the constant flow of answers that continue to spew out of my mouth like a crack in a dam wall.

Blaze pulls me into his embrace, wrapping both strong arms around me, and holds me snug against his muscular chest. He rubs a circle on my back between my shoulder blades. "There, there, you're alright," he says with a voice that would calm the wildest of beasts, including the one inside of me.

He's my boyfriend again. At least it feels that way to me. I breathe in the scent of him that is so unique and soothes my nerves. No amount of tincture could affect me this well. My thoughts slow and settle like a calm after a storm. My heart slows to a more reasonable pace, and my breath no longer feels like I'm on the verge of hyperventilating. I feel a sense of control again, and I sigh.

He continues to hold me. Not saying anything, just holding me. I like it here in his arms. All is right with the world here. Barkley rubs up against my leg, but I don't move. I feel the dog circle us. Maybe he's wanting in on this loving moment. But I don't want to move. This is heaven. A safe place to be.

A knock hits the door as if an eagle lost its sense of direction and flew into my door. I jump so hard my teeth slam together. "Ow! I bit my tongue."

Barkley lowers his front end and growls toward the noise.

I stagger away from Blaze— or did he shove me? He has one hand hovering over where I know he holsters his gun and the other in front of himself, as if to push whoever is at the door back away from us.

The door flies opens and two men spill into my foyer. They are carrying cases and boxes and are both panting. Blaze's posture relaxes. Barkley wags his tail. My heart is still in my throat and pounding like a toy monkey on steroids beating a drum.

My brain recognizes the men. Slowly my heart and lungs react appropriately. Joe and Matt, Blaze's detective partners. I know them from the raid, and better from moving Abbie's furniture. They are here to help stop Donald.

"Good, you're here." Blaze says. "Where'd you park?"

Joe shoves a thumb over his shoulder. "Matt drove." He sets a briefcase that could easily be a suitcase full of clothes, but I know it's equipment, and a box down on the tile. Then he turns to Matt who is doing the same with his cases.

Matt nods. "Yeah, I parked in your garage and closed the door."

"Good."

"Let's get set up in the dining room." He gestures for Joe to bring the paraphernalia.

"Hi, Maribeth." Joe says casually as he walks past me. If I didn't know better, I'd think he was here for a movie night and just brought the popcorn and tequila.

"Hey." I say, coming out of my terrified fog.

"Heard you anticipate trouble with that Conway fella." Matt states conversationally as he draws out a devise that looks like a laptop computer.

"Yeah, some." I stammer.

"Let me see your cell phone." Blaze holds out his hand toward me.

"Why?" I blink.

"We're going to connect this doohickey so we can all hear when Conway calls," Blaze says.

"Actually," Matt smiles at Blaze like he's a moron. "It's an app that I will install. We can tap into your calls from the laptop and record, also. Once we've figured out what Conway's up to, I'll delete it from your phone, promise." He holds up his hand just like he would if he were standing in front of a judge, swearing to tell the truth, the whole truth, and nothing else.

I tilt my head. "Why do I suddenly feel all sorts of conspiracy alarms going off in my head?"

"Oh, sweetheart," Blaze reaches for me with a smile."You know you can trust these guys. They're my partners."

I push his hands away. "I feel very vulnerable right now. No, I don't know I can trust anybody right now."

Barkley barks as if to remind me he is there. I look down. He has taken on a protective stance between me and the men. "Except Barkley." I say. "I know I can trust him!"

A smile creeps onto my lips. I look at the guys, hoping they understand how scared I am, and that I don't mean them any disrespect. Matt hands me my phone back and opens the laptop. He is logging in and setting something up, plugging in a set of headphones, and creating a file. He hands Blaze and Joe a wireless earbud. They will be able to listen when Donald calls and I can record everything at the same time.

"That's cool. Scary, but cool." I say.

Joe laughs. "Don't worry, Miss, we're with the government and we're here to help."

He winks at me. Matt frowns at Joe. "Seriously, Maribeth, we only do this when we are after bad guys. We'd never do anything like this to an ordinary citizen."

I nod. Wrestling with the child inside my head who is crying and curled up in a ball.

Blaze rolls his eyes. "Stop apologizing for doing your job. If it weren't for this surveillance app, we'd be up sh—"

My phone rings.

I jump and squeak a little, then whisper, "What do I do? What do I do?" I wave my hands like a little bird about to fall off my branch.

Blaze quickly inserts the bud in his ear canal and whispers. "Just answer it like you always do."

Suddenly my mind goes blank. How do I answer my phone? Say hello? Give my name. I look at the screen. It's Abbie. I sigh.

"It's just Abbie." I say in a normal volume.

A huge sigh ripples among the men. Matt disconnects the call from his laptop. I answer, "Hey Abbie, how are you?"

"I'm fine." She says curtly.

My brow furrows. "Everything okay?"

"Sure. Great. I-I need to see you," she says.

"Something's wrong." I mouth to the guys while pointing at my phone.

Matt scrambles to reconnect the call to the program, and Blaze and Joe touch their ear buds.

Blaze writes quickly on a pad and holds it up in front of me. "Is Conway with her?"

Oh God! Could he have kidnapped my friend and be holding her to get what he wants from me? She was acting very strange.

"Abbie?" I try to think of some way to ask her if she's in trouble. An idea comes to me. In lieu of pig latin, we have computer language to use for code. God, I hope this works. I say, "Did you get those meta tags for me like I asked?"

It's a great question for code speak. As long as Donald doesn't know anything about HTML programming, this should work. Hopefully, she can use that as a way to let me know if something is wrong.

"I have them right here. Right in front of me." She says, emphasizing the last sentence.

I whip my head toward Matt. My eyes are excitedly wide. "He's with her!" I mouth then continue talking to Abbie. "Good. So, can I come by and pick them up?"

"I, uh." She hesitates. "That would be great. Besides, we need to talk about other things anyway."

"Blaze and I were just about to go out for dinner, we can stop by." I want her to know Blaze will come too and she will be safe.

"No! Come alone." She sounds shaken, like someone shook her. "I mean, uh…"

"Oh, I see," I say. "So we need to have a *girl* talk, huh?"

"Exactly." She sounds relieved.

"Okay, I'll explain to Blaze, he'll understand. I'll see you in a little bit," I say. "You be careful. I'll be right over."

I hope she understands that I won't let Donald hurt her in any way if I can help it. Reluctantly, I hang up. I hate losing the connection with her. As long as I had her on the phone, I know she's okay. The minute I hung up, I have no idea what Donald will do to her. My gut clenches. I feel nauseous. "He's got her! I'm sure of it."

Matt nods. "Yeah, we got that. No one hands you a meta tag." He chuckles. "Clever girl."

Blaze's forehead bears down with his brows. "I don't get it."

"It's HTML code. One writes meta tags, or metadata when one writes in Hypertext Markup Language, like for a website. Metadata summarizes basic information about the data. It makes a website, for example, easier to find. It's not anything physical that can be handed to another person." I explain.

He tilts his head back and mouths, "Oh."

"Abbie's a genius, actually." I tell him.

"So are you," Blaze says pushing his chest out like a rooster?

I narrow my gaze on him. "So, what are we going to do? I have to go alone or he'll kill her, I'm sure of it."

Blaze and his cohorts glance at each other. "We've got a plan."

Chapter Eleven

"I wish it was winter," I say for the umpteenth time. "I could wear more clothes, you know? A big, oversized sweater."

I'm positive Blaze and his fellow detectives are tired of hearing me rattle on and on about this. Apparently, I have no control over my thoughts that spill out my mouth when I'm out-of-my-mind terrified. In this late-May heat, I can only wear one layer of clothing during daylight hours. Jeans and a t-shirt won't be conspicuous when I go into Abbie's house and confront Donald or whoever else is there holding my friend hostage. Why can't the weather cooperate with our endeavor and give me a nice chilly cold spell?

"You *sure* the wire won't show?" I ask, again.

"Positive." Matt assures me for an equal amount of umpteenth times. He glances at Blaze, who is the one putting the wire in place, and then Matt looks into my eyes. "Maribeth, you've changed bras three times. I promise you this one with the extra padding in the cup for a lift-effect is thick enough to completely hide the device." Now that's hilarious!

A blush heats my cheeks. I want so bad to cover my face with my hands. But I stand straight like a good soldier, and let Blaze get everything just right. Granted, the "device" is thin and flesh colored, and it all goes inside my bra cup, I can't help but feel like it is protruding somehow. I just know Donald or his goon will notice right away. It's about the size of a key fob battery. It feels like I've put a dime on the side of my breast for safe keeping. The ultra-thin wire runs along the underwire of the bra and clips to the front like a cute little bow.

All bras have bows. It's nothing unusual. If Donald's goons pat me down, they'll never know I am wearing a two-way listening device. My breasts are squished together and peeking over the top, thanks to the padding insert. If my cleavage exposure does the trick the way it's supposed to when clubbing, perhaps Donald or his goon's eyes won't get any further down my shirt than the scoop neck.

But I feel like it has a neon light flashing from underneath my t-shirt. They will know instantly that I'm wired, and that one man is parked nearby so he can hear every word said and two others are sneaking up to be ready to bust into Abbie's house when they have what they need to arrest them.

"There. How's that feel?" Matt steps back from Blaze's handiwork. Looking at me as if he has just watched his cohort dress a mannequin for a special display. His eyes rove over my chest, confirming nothing looks out of place, or sticking out inappropriately.

"Like I'm gonna die the minute I walk into that house." I grumble. "Ah, I wish it was winter…"

"We know!" Joe smirks. "It's going to be okay. Just put on that poker face that you do so well, and you'll do fine."

Blaze takes me by the shoulders and looks deeply into my eyes. "You said it yourself. He's playing a game. You're excellent at games. You can do this." He kisses my forehead.

I breathe in deeply and let it out. "But… I've never played for someone else's life. If anything happens to Abbie—"

"It won't. We will be right there." Matt says.

"Trust us…" Joe smiles an ornery grin. "We are professionals."

I squint a sideways glare at him. It's his joke and I get it, but I'm just not in a joking mood. "I want to trust you guys. Honest I do."

I rub my temples, easing the migraine that is threatening to turn my grey matter into goo. "It's just, I've never done anything like this before. I mean, up until a few weeks ago, I thought Donald Conway was my dad's bff. Now, I think he had everything to do with my dad's suicide… somehow. He may want to kill me, too."

I scan three empathetic faces. Blaze has a worried shadow behind a set jaw. He's acting as though he has no doubts, but I sense he is very concerned. I am too.

But I'm more concerned for Abbie's life. I have to do this. I just hope I don't get us both killed.

"I don't know how or why Donald caused my father's death. It's a feeling I have, otherwise why would he keep insisting we 'talk' about it?"

Blaze pulls me close. "He had big plans for taking over the underground gambling here in Deadwood." Blaze rests his arm across my shoulders. "For some criminals, that's enough to destroy lives. We raided the game the very night he attempted to take over. It was a coincidence, but he doesn't know that. He may hold you responsible for the sleight of hand that foiled his game. For that, I'm sorry." He touches his forehead to mine as if he could press his confidence into my brain. He looks directly in my eyes. "Maribeth, I had no idea you were involved. I, we, would have done things differently if we knew."

The sincerity in Blaze's voice and his eyes warms my heart down to my toes. I purse a smile. I nod. Steeling myself for what I've got to do to save Abbie. It's all about Abbie now.

"Okay. Let's ante up and get this game started." I say.

I drive Kiley, and the boys follow in Matt's discrete Chevy Silverado with ultra dark tinted windows on the side and back. I park in Abbie's driveway, they park nearby and set up their surveillance in the cab of the pickup. Blaze and Joe will circle through the backyards and come in, hopefully, unnoticed.

My hands are shaking as I turn Kiley's growling engine off. The time it took to drive here dissolved my steeled backbone. I squeeze my fingers tight, trying to still the tremor. Closing my eyes, I visualize a large, round, green felt-covered table. Red, blue, and white chips stacked in front of me. The smell of a freshly opened deck of cards. The flutter of the shuffle machine. The dealer's voice as he tosses out each card. The settling feeling that happens in my mind as I lift my cards to view my hand for the first time. No reaction. I look up.

"I'm ready." I say out loud.

I get out of my precious Kiley, glancing back as if this might be the last time I see her but I'm okay with that, and walk to Abbie's door. This is for Abbie. Lifting my hand to knock, the door pops open. My poker face slips a millisecond, but I scramble to put it back in place, and I smile.

"Hey." Abbie says with a friendly tone, but her face reflects a whole other deck of emotions.

"Hey." I give her a little nod to assure her everything is alright. "You got those meta tags for me?"

"Uh, sure do." She steps back. Or more like she is jerked back.

My jaw drops as I lunge forward to grab her wrist.

"Abbie!" I gasp. "You alri—"

Then I see Donald. "You!"

I make sure my friend has regained her balance before I address the monster to my right. "What on earth are you doing here, Donald?" I feign surprise. "Needing a website? Brutes R Us?"

He smiles.

Oil slithers over my tongue, giving me a rancid taste in my mouth. I hate this man. I resist the gag at the back of my throat. "I thought you skipped town? I heard your bail bondsman is sending a bounty hunter out looking for you."

His smile widens. "Turns out my bail bondsman was looking to retire. We worked a deal."

"You bribed a bail—" I narrow my eyes on him. Only Donald would have the gumption to bribe a bail bondsman and get away with it. "How convenient." I step further inside Abbie's house. She looks pale and terrified. I try using my special-eye-contact superpower to convey to her everything will be alright, but it doesn't seem to be working today. "So, is this where you want to talk to me? About Dad?"

"Seems like as good a place as any." Donald says.

I want to punch him in the face and break all the teeth in that cocky smile of his. I visualize a jagged, broken smile with blood running down his chin. "Okay. Let's talk." I glance at Abbie. I've got to do something to get her out of here. "But first, why not let Abbie go pick us up some Starbucks' coffees? I sure could use one, how about you?"

I glance at Abbie with a reassuring smile then back to Donald. Over his shoulder, I see his shadow goon, standing at attention. I almost wish I'd brought Barkley. I could just make a hand gesture and send the dog to attack the goon-in-waiting, while I slam something into Donald's face.

I divert my eyes quickly, looking for such an object to use as my battering ram. There is a glass ashtray that I recall was pretty heavy when we placed it on a table beside the door.

Abbie inherited it from her grandfather who smoked cigars. She is now using it to hold her car keys when she comes in the door. I could do some damage with that ashtray, but I know the sentimental value of it to Abbie. I glance around some more.

"What are you looking for, girly?" Donald growls.

"Don't call me girly!" I snap my attention back to him. "I'm admiring how good Abbie's place turned out after our declutter." I glance toward her. "It really looks adorable." I say conversationally.

She smiles, but it's not a happy smile.

I'm just trying to distract Donald until Blaze and Joe come crashing in. However, I haven't given them any reason to come crashing in. I need to get Donald to tell me what he's up to without him figuring out I have a team of detectives listening to everything we say. So far, all he's done is make my girlfriend very uncomfortable and forced her to call me to come over. Not exactly prison worthy. I narrow my eyes at Donald.

"What do you want, *Conway*?" His name leaves a terrible taste in my mouth.

"I told you, I want to talk about your dad." Donald says. He gestures for us to go sit down in Abbie's living room.

Poor Abbie. She looks like she's about to pass out. I turn my full attention to her. The blanched pallor of her face gives me an idea.

"Do you need something to eat?" I say. My mind is rolling like a freight train without brakes. I hope this works to make Donald let Abbie leave this house while he is doing whatever this is he's doing.

"Is your blood sugar too low?" I act like I am frantically searching on every surface in her entry and living room. "Where's your meter. Have you tested your blood?"

I turn to Donald. "She's diabetic, you buffoon. Has she had anything to eat while you've been here?"

"No." Donald actually looks concerned. This almost gives me pause and certainly hope. Maybe this is working. I touch her forehead. While I'm so close to her face, I whisper, "Play along."

"She looks awful!" I stand and whirl around to face Donald. "We need to call an ambulance! She could go into a diabetic coma!" Using the terms I heard when Big Mike really was having a diabetic incident. I glare at Abbie. She gets it and closes her eyes. "See! She's passing out!"

I lift my phone, giving Donald a daring glare. I'm not sure if I should actually call 911 or what, but I've gotta follow through somehow. I dial it and wait.

When they answer I tell them the address and that my friend is having some sort of diabetic episode." It's the best I can do at the moment. At least it will stall Donald and get Abbie out of the house. The emergency dispatcher asks another question, but I hang up.

I cross my fingers in hope that this will get Abbie out of here, as I collapse next to her and rub my knuckles on her chest, like I'm trying to revive her. "Stay with me, Abbie."

Donald sits while his goon continues to stand at attention just a few feet away from his master.

Soon, we hear the siren. I continue to hold Abbie in my lap and coo encouraging things to her. The siren hesitates, as if they turned it off, but then it starts up again. At last, they are in her driveway. They seem to take forever to get out of the vehicle, then they come to the door. I turn to Donald and gesture with my head for him to open the door.

He glares at me. "Go ahead, you're closer."

I wriggle out from under Abbie, and gently put her head down to the floor, then open the door. "Thank God, you're here!" I say.

"Yeah, dispatch says you've got a person having a diabetic episode." The EMT looks past me to Abbie who is sprawled on the floor. "Yep," he says and pushes past me.

The two of them surround Abbie, bringing with them a back board while a third, a woman, stays outside with a gurney. The first guy squats beside her and says something I cannot hear. They press something against her forearm. It looks like a laser gun. "Yeah, her blood sugar is 30." The guy announces loudly. "Let's work fast."

"Really?" I blurt before I think about what I'm saying. Was it a coincidence her blood sugar really had dipped so low?

He pulls out a plastic bag and holds it in the air over Abbie's face. The other guy works in front of his body where I cannot see what he's doing, but when he is done, the tube from the plastic bag is taped to Abbie's wrist. They turn her onto her side, slide the board under her back, roll her onto the board, strap her down quickly, and lift her with a chant, "One, two, three."

"Good thing you called when you did, Miss." The guy says to me loudly. I assume he's speaking so loud because his adrenaline is coursing and he doesn't realize how high his volume is.

I nod.

"Thank you," I say as I watch them take my friend to the ambulance. I have no idea how many laws we have broken by faking that emergency. Or was it real? He said her blood sugar was 30. My god, she could really be going into a coma is that were true?

But at least Abbie is out of danger from Donald. The men quickly jump into their places in the ambulance. The siren screams as it fades toward the hospital.

I turn to find Donald and his goon standing. I swallow. "Wow, that was crazy, huh?"

"Sit down, Maribeth." Donald says sternly.

I move to sit in a chair that faces the coffee table centered with the couch where Donald sits. His goon positions himself at the sliding glass door leading into Abbie's back garden. I hope the glass door is where Blaze and Joe will crash through and take that monkey down first thing.

"Now that the theatrics are over, let's talk." Donald speaks slowly.

I feign innocence, but I know the jig is up. My bluff is being called and it's time to lay my cards on the table. "Okay, fine. What is it, Donald? What's so important you had to take my girlfriend hostage to get me here?"

"Your father."

"What about my father?" I lift my chin a notch.

"There's something you need to know?" He laces his fingers together and leans his elbows on to his knees.

"Oh really? And just what about my father do I need to know?"

"He committed suicide… as an act of retaliation. He thought he could sever the ties that bound him to me. It was a foolish attempt to save your mother and you."

I stare at him. "Save us from what?"

He grins wickedly. "Me."

Chapter Twelve

"Are you getting this." Blaze steps out of the backseat of the pickup truck, leaning in the open driver's side window. His eyes flicker from Matt to the direction of Abbie's house. Matt parked several houses away from Abbie where his truck could not be seen by anyone in the house. They sat in the truck while Maribeth first entered. Once she called 9-1-1, they continued to wait since Conway wasn't going to reveal anything while that was happening. But they continued to listen.

"Ten-four." Matt replies without looking up from his laptop in the passenger seat.

"Now we can get to the nitty gritty of what this ape is planning." Joe says, standing with his back to Blaze, as if he were watching for trouble behind him.

Abbie walks up to the pickup truck with a small can of orange juice in her hand and gets into the back seat. There are too many devices in the front seat of the detective's truck for her to sit next to him. The ambulance makes a u-turn and quietly drives away.

"Is Maribeth alright?" she asks as she settles in the back.

"Yeah," Matt turns to speak over his shoulder. "How was your ambulance ride?" He smiles.

"They were very nice. Drove me all the way to the hospital so the sirens wouldn't give anything away. Then drove me back here, sans the sirens."

"Good." Matt looks at her with a tilt of his head and a frown. "I don't have another set of earphones, but since we are out here, I can take mine off, redirect the audio to the computer's speakers, and let you ear what's going on."

"Thank you. Will Blaze and Joe still be able to hear?" She leans over the seat to look at the computer screen.

"Sure, they have bluetooth ear buds."

Abbie nods with a sigh. "Has that guy said anything good yet?"

"No, actually they're just getting started. Don't worry, Blaze and Joe are gonna get into position" —Matt glares at Blaze, signaling him to move —"and will be ready to enter as soon as we have enough evidence." Matt assures Abbie.

"Just make sure you don't wait too long. Maribeth is a good friend, and I'd hate to lose her to something as asinine as that gorilla."

"We won't." Blaze pats the open window. "You alright?" He asks Abbie.

"Yeah, that was brilliant." A half smile breaks the taut line on her lips. "How'd you guys get an actual ambulance to fake an emergency for me?"

"Maribeth called 9-1-1 for real," Blaze says. "We intercepted them before they got to your house and told them what was going down. They did a superb job of getting you outta there, huh?"

"I'll say. Taping an IV tube to my arm was the *pièce de résistance*. I was impressed." A slight giggle escaped her mouth.

"Well, I'm just glad you're alright." Blaze pats the open window again. He turns to Matt. "We gotta go."

Matt nodded.

I laugh nervously. What could Donald mean? My father died in an attempt to save Momma and me… from Donald? How? I don't understand. My mind reels, trying to make sense of this nonsense. I suspect Donald had something to do with my dad's death, but this is throwing me for a loop. I shake my head. "What are you saying?"

Donald takes a deep breath and settles back into the couch. "Well, it all started long ago, before you were born. Your father had a problem. A problem that cost him a lot of money. But he couldn't walk away from his problem."

"Stop talking like you're telling me a fairy tale. What was this problem my dad had?"

Donald paused. His eyes fixed on mine. "He was addicted to gambling. He was good, but not every game ended in his favor."

He let that sink into my brain and then continued. "And he owed a lot of money to the gamers to whom he had lost." He took an exaggerated inhale, reminding me of Alfred Hitchcock before each movie's beginning. "That's where I came in. Or rather, he came to me. I loaned him the money to get square with the gaming room." His eyebrows slowly lifted on his forehead. "At a reasonable interest rate, accrued at a reasonable pace."

I tilted my head. "I'm sure you were very *reasonable* as a loan shark. Seeings how you're so reasonable as a gaming host." The sarcasm oozed from my words like putrid, green slime.

Donald's smile grew uglier. "May I remind you, your father, much like yourself, came to me requesting my help." He splayed his finger over his chest. "Not the other way around."

"May I remind you," I say. "I was under the mistaken idea that you were my father's best friend. When I asked you for help that first time." I huffed. "Some friend you turned out to be."

His brow lifted same as his shoulder in a shrug.

I leaned toward him. "I thought I could trust you!"

Tears burned in my eyes. I gritted my teeth. *I will not cry!* I chanted to myself. "Okay, so, my dad owed you money? What's the big deal about that?" I sit back in the chair. "What's so freaking special about that for you to tell me that my father killed himself to save us… from you? I don't see how the dots connect."

"Come on. You're a very intelligent woman. You know how the game is played. You need money, you have no resources to borrow the money, so you go to a source that is willing to lend you money, at a reasonable interest, since you are now considered a high risk. You use the money but Lady Luck isn't your friend so you lose. Now you owe money you cannot repay but… the interest continued to accrue. Before long, unless you miraculously win the big jackpot, you get further and further behind until there is nothing else you can do but put up everything you own… along with your family for collateral."

He sat back and took a deep breath.

I stare at him, letting his tale sink into my brain that is hurting more and more with each tick of the oversized clock on Abbie's wall. It's as if each tick tightens a vise around my head. The pain presses down on the part of my brain that allows me to put together the pieces Donald is dealing. Did he say my own father used Momma and me for collateral to get more money?

"Wait." I suddenly connect a few dots but they aren't making clear picture. "My daddy wasn't a loser. He was a genius. He won every game…" I mutter to myself, "like I do."

I fold my hands in my lap. "Were you skimming a profit off his winnings, like you said you were doing from my winnings? Was he in one of your seats?"

Donald nods with a smug look of satisfaction on his face.

Whenever I requested to sit at a high stakes table in Denver, I was always allowed in because, unbeknownst to me, Donald had pre-paid seats for his puppets. He automatically received a portion of their winnings and because they were in one of his seats, they always won.

"Then…" My brain is struggling to keep up. "How could he lose? That last time, how could he lose if he was in a chair Donald controlled?" I glare at Donald.

"You turned sixteen."

My brow draws together, squeezing the pain tighter in my head. What did that mean? What did me turning sixteen have to do with Daddy losing? I let the thought run through my head… what did it mean?

"Oh my God!" I get it. Donald bargained with my daddy to use me and Momma as collateral and in turn Donald, the man who I thought for all my life was my Daddy's best friend, I called him Uncle, because I thought he and Daddy were so close, like brothers, but in truth he was… he was daddy's… I can barely say the word, even in my head. "Handler." And Momma and I were on the verge of being used for prostitution.

Nausea hits me hard. I breathe quickly through my nose, trying to stay the contents of my stomach from spewing across Abbie's cute area rug.

"So… you were going to… force me… and Momma to work for you? You're a pimp, too?"

He smiled. "Now you're tuning in to reality, Maribeth."

"So," I'm hoping this is enough information for Blaze and Joe to come crashing in. "You're telling me, not only were you a loan shark, a handler for poker players, and God knows what else, but you had a human trafficking side-gig for when your 'loan customers' couldn't pay their debt. Which, of course, all of them would end up that way with your 'reasonable' interest rates that probably accrued daily. Am I right?"

No one is crashing through the doors or windows! I am terrified I haven't made him say enough. What else do they need? I look toward the goon standing in front of the sliding glass door. I see a shadow. Blaze is there. Why doesn't he come in? Maybe they need more, but what?

I look at Donald's smug face. I want, so badly, to smash him in the face with that ashtray, sentimental or not, Donald needs to be taken down a notch, or two. "Well? Am I right?"

He tilts his head with a smile. "Remember, you came to me. After your father died, you came to me and asked for my help. Because you came to me, I have you under my thumb, Maribeth. Your father's debt will never be paid. Neither will yours."

"Mine!" I yell. "When did I borrow a dime from you?"

"Not a dime. But my favor. Remember you came into an adult game when you were only sixteen. Underage. And yet you begged me to let you play. You won. Remember. And you won every game you entered after that one. My good graces helped you return to a lifestyle you preferred living." His smile widened.

"You?" I interrupt. "You did all that? You fixed the games, what about all those other people who lost to my miraculous winnings? What happened to them?"

"Yes, I did, but they are not your concern."

"Why not?" I scoot to the edge of my chair. "Who did they put up for collateral to be in the game? Did they put their family into your evil human trafficking gig?" Tears stream from my eyes. I can no longer hold them back.

"It's a game, Maribeth. One never knows who will win. It's up to the fates." He shrugs, holding his palms out. "Consequences are consequences. The chips fall where they fall."

"What does that even mean?"

He leaned forward. An evil mask washed over his face. "It means, Maribeth, when your father sold his soul to me, he sold your soul as well. You, my dear, are mine to do with as I please."

I swallow the nausea back. "Then, why did you continue to let me play poker, rather… rather than put me to work on the streets."

"Because you really were good at it, like your father, you had a mind for math and counting cards. I made much more from having you play poker."

My eyes narrow. "How much more do you need?" I say, exasperated over Blaze's hesitation.

"What do you mean?" Donald's brow furrows.

The sliding glass door jerks open. "Police! Don't move." Blaze shouts.

The front door opens, Joe rushes in. "Police! Show me your hands!"

The goon turns, pulling out a gun from under his jacket. Blaze points his pistol at the man's forehead. "Don't do it."

Donald casually lifts his hands in surrender.

I come to my feet. "What took you so long!"

"I'm sorry." Blaze slaps handcuffs on the goon's wrists behind his back. "Let's go."

Joe has cuffed Donald and is guiding him toward the front door.

Donald turns to speak over his shoulder. "You're mine, Maribeth. Nothing they charge me with will stick, trust me. I have lawyers at my disposal, the law can't touch me." He laughs.

"Well, I'm touching you now." Joe growls as he shoves Donald across the threshold. Two police cars sit in the driveway.

When did they arrive?

Uniformed officers take Donald, then the goon and gingerly place them in the backseat of each sedan. They drive away. Blaze and Joe stroll back into Abbie's house.

"Holy Moly, why did you take so long?" I yell at Blaze.

He smiles and walks straight to me, gathering me into his arms. "Well, for one, we were getting as much out of Conway as we could, and for two, we were waiting for the mobile units to arrive so that once we had Conway and his body guard, we'd have a place to put them."

I slug Blaze on the shoulder. "Next time let a girl know what's going on."

He chuckles. "What's this 'next time'? And as crazy as you were about wearing a wire in your bra, how could you have worn a listening device in your ear and not wigged out about them finding it?"

I still. "You're right." I look up at him. "Just kiss me."

Blaze grins then lowers his lips near to mine. He hovers there, mere inches from my mouth.

"Yes ma'am," he breathes the words. I feel the warmth of his breath across my mouth. And then he kisses me.

Donald is wrong. I am not his to do with as he wishes. I am Blaze's and he is mine. I look into his eyes when we come up for air.

"I love you." I say.

He smiles. "I love you, too."

THE END

Love the story?
Leave a review.

Next book is Winner Takes All in Deadwood

About the Author

 Lynn Donovan is an author, playwright, and director who spends her days chasing after her muses trying to get them to behave long enough to write their stories. The results are numerous novels, multi-author series, anthologies, dramatizations, and short stories.

Lynn enjoys reading and writing all kinds of fiction, historical western romance, paranormal, speculative, contemporary romance, and time travel. But you never know what her muses will come up with for a story, so you could see a novel under any given genre. All that can be said is keep your eyes open, because these muses are not sitting still for long!

Oops, there they go again…

Want more?

You can learn more about Lynn when you follow her on her Facebook Author Page at https://www.facebook.com/LynnDonovanAuthor, join her reading group on FB at Books by Author Lynn Donovan @ https://www.facebook.com/groups/BooksbyAuthorLynnDonovan/, her website LynnDonovanAuthor.com and Twitter @MLynnDonovan,

For more publications by Lynn Donovan go to: Amazon.com/author/ldonovan

Newsletter and a Free Gift for You

Hey! Thank you for purchasing and reading this book. I'd like to give you a parting gift to show my appreciation. Sign up for my newsletter at lynndonovanauthor.com/newsletter. I will send you an e-copy of a collection of short stories I wrote purely for your entertainment. I will happily send you this e-copy for FREE, if you ask. I will also add you to my NEWSLETTER list and you will receive up-to-date information on new release before anyone else.

This book will **not** be sold anywhere, at any time, I am keeping it exclusively for you, my readers, and only if you ask for it.

Thank you again, and God Bless.

~Lynn Donovan

Milton Keynes UK
Ingram Content Group UK Ltd.
UKHW011946160224
437951UK00001B/32

9 798224 578139